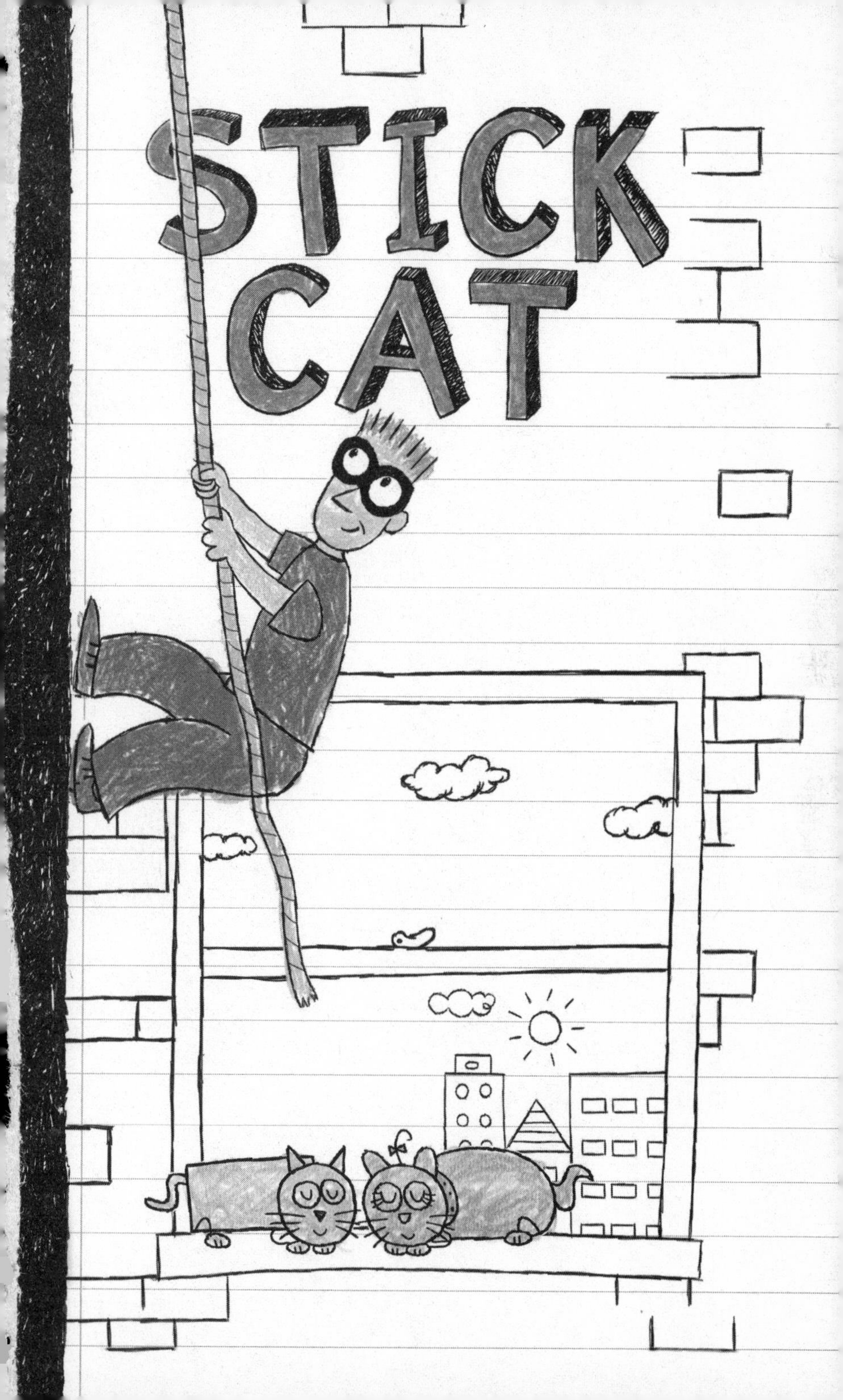
STICK
CAT

STICK CAT

By Tom Watson

Two Catch a Thief

HARPER

An Imprint of HarperCollinsPublishers

Library of Congress Control Number: 2017932856
ISBN 978-0-06-241104-4

Typography by Jeff Shake
17 18 19 20 21 CG/LSCH 10 9 8 7 6 5 4 3 2 1
❖
First Edition

To K8
(And Morris)

Table of Contents

Chapter 1

THE SWEETHEART DANCE

Umm, okay.

You're not going to believe this. I'm not even sure I believe it myself.

It's Sweetheart Dance time at my school. Do you know what that means? It's February and the gym gets transformed into a red, white, and pink lovey-dovey romance-a-torium.

SWEETHEART DANCE!

It's gross.

Totally sickening.

1

But do you know who's not gross?

Mary Cunningham.

And do you know what's *not* sickening?

I'm pretty sure she's into me.

Well, maybe not *into* me.

But she doesn't ignore me. And she does talk to me. She even sat down by me at lunch in the cafeteria a couple of days ago.

I'm not making that up. It wasn't a dream. It definitely happened.

I was there.

You remember who she is, right? Mary?

How can I put this?

Umm.

She's cute.

MARY = CUTE

There. I said it. As long as she doesn't find out I think that, everything's cool.

So don't tell her.

She also likes cats. And I don't mean she just has a cat for a pet. She actually has two. But I don't mean she just has two cats either.

What I mean is Mary is crazy about cats. You know, obsessed. She has cats all over the place. On folders, book covers, pencils, sweaters, everything.

This combination—Mary being, you know, cute combined with her cat obsession—made me want to write the first Stick Cat story.

I usually write Stick Dog stories in my English class, but then the whole suddenly-I'm-noticing-Mary thing happened. That's when I wrote a Stick Cat story to get her attention.

And I got it—her attention.

She liked that first story about Stick Cat and his best friend, Edith, a lot. In that story, they went on a rescue mission to save Mr. Music.

Mary liked the second story even more. In that one, Stick Cat and Edith helped Hazel, an old woman who made bagels.

And now, just today, she sat down next to me at lunch.

I know, right?

Unbelievable.

This is what happened.

First, she opened her lunchbox. Guess what? It had a cat on it. Shocking, right?

She unwrapped her PB&J and said, "Did you hear about the Sweetheart Dance?"

After almost gagging on a gulp of chocolate

milk, I answered, "I saw the posters in the hallway."

Mary, after deciding that my milk drinking did not, in fact, demand the Heimlich maneuver, added, "It's where the girls ask the boys instead of the other way around."

When she said this, I made the brilliant decision to not eat or drink anything for the rest of lunch. This, I knew, would keep my choking to death to a minimum.

Do you know what an "awkward silence" is?

It's what happens when there's a totally obvious subject between two people who are both thinking the same thing—but neither one of them has the courage to say anything.

That kind of silence happened today at the lunch table with me and Mary. She took a few nibbles of her PB&J. And I continued to not eat and not choke in a very macho and natural way.

Mary finally broke the silence.

She asked, "Are you working on another Stick Cat story?"

This was a brilliant move on her part. She had brought up the whole Sweetheart Dance subject but hadn't asked me or anything.

Not yet.

"I'm thinking about writing another one."

"Can I be the first to read it?"

I nodded.

Mary smiled.

And I was totally thankful for three things.

1. Mary sat by me at lunch today.

2. I didn't choke to death.

3. English class was right after lunch.

Chapter 2

LESS STUCK THAN USUAL

Stick Cat's roommate, Goose, had already left for work. And Stick Cat rested on the windowsill of their apartment on the twenty-third floor.

The big city was wide-awake now. Stick Cat had already watched the sun's reflection brighten thousands of windows among the dozens of buildings he could see.

It was the time of day that Stick Cat enjoyed most. And it was not just because he loved how the city slowly illuminated as the morning progressed.

9

It was also because he knew it was simply a matter of time before his best friend, Edith, would call for him.

He closed his eyes and waited.

For six seconds.

"Stick Cat!"

STICK CAT!

It was Edith.

Stick Cat opened his eyes, hopped down to the living room floor, and began to pad his way across the soft, plush carpet toward the bathroom.

"Stick Cat!"

"Coming," he called back.

He was nearly to the bathroom now. It was where he met Edith almost every day. They had scratched a hole in the wall that separated their two apartments from each other.

The hole was concealed in their respective bathroom cabinets. It had never been discovered by Goose or by Edith's roommate, Tiffany.

"Stick Cat!"

"Almost there," he said. He was in the bathroom now.

"I've got great news!" called Edith. Stick Cat could hear true excitement in her voice.

Stick Cat opened the cabinet door and saw exactly what he expected.

Edith was stuck in the wall.

He didn't comment about her predicament at all. He knew better than to do that. Instead, he asked, "What's your good news?"

"I'm less stuck than usual!" exclaimed Edith. "Isn't that terrific?"

"I suppose," answered Stick Cat. Something seemed to bother him though—like something didn't make sense to him. Stick

Cat hesitated a moment before asking, "But aren't you either stuck or not stuck? I'm not sure there can be degrees of stuck-ness."

"Of course there can," Edith said. She seemed almost offended at Stick Cat's suggestion. "Yesterday, I was totally jammed in here. Remember? I seemed to get caught right at my tummy for some reason. I'm not sure why. My midsection is one of my most attractive and elegant feline features."

Edith stopped speaking then and just stared at Stick Cat. She appeared to be waiting for something. After several seconds, she added, "Wouldn't you agree?"

"Agree with what?" Stick Cat asked. He had honestly forgotten what she might be referring to.

"That my belly is one of my most attractive and elegant feline features."

"Oh, yes," Stick Cat said as fast as he could. He had quickly realized the proper course of action. "Without question."

"I knew you'd agree," Edith went on. "Why I got stuck there I have no idea. Remember how it took you almost twenty pulls to get me out?"

"I remember," answered Stick Cat. He rotated his shoulders a little bit to loosen them up. They were still sore.

"Well, now look!" Edith said. You could tell that she wanted to share her good news with Stick Cat. "Now my tummy is through, but my hips are stuck. That's a lot better, don't you think?"

"I guess so." Stick Cat was clearly not very convinced.

"I just think that's so much better, don't you?"

This time, Stick Cat did not hesitate at all. "So much better. Totally. Yes."

There was a moment of silence between them again.

Ultimately, Edith said, "Well, are you going to pull me out or what?"

Stick Cat reached for her paws, clasped them with his own, and began the task.

"I'll keep count," Edith commented.

After five pulls, she hadn't budged at all.

"Stick Cat?"

"Yes?" he answered. He was happy to have
a reason to take a break.

"You're yanking a little too hard," said Edith.
"You're, like, jerking or something. Try
to just pull with a more consistent effort
instead of stopping and starting so much."

Stick Cat squeezed his lips together. He
made no response to this suggestion at all
and began to pull with a more consistent
effort.

Edith didn't budge.

"Stick Cat?"

"Yes?" He had pulled on her eleven times now. He was pleased to get another break.

"I'm getting tired."

"*You're* getting tired?"

"That's right," Edith answered. "It's not easy being stuck in a wall, let me tell you."

"I, umm, wouldn't know."

"Well, holding still like this in one position can be frustrating. And I get a little sore too. Yesterday, I was sore around my belly.

Today, my hips are getting sore."

"I see," Stick Cat said—mainly because he couldn't think of anything else to say.

"So, I was just wondering."

"Yes?"

"Could you speed this along a bit?"

Stick Cat did not answer, but he did pull at Edith six more times.

"Stop," Edith sighed. "That's seventeen pulls and you're not making any progress."

"Yeah, I know."

"No offense, Stick Cat," Edith said, and

looked at him directly. "But maybe you should start exercising or something."

"Excuse me?"

"You know, working out," Edith explained further. "I mean, it seems to take you longer and longer to get me out of the wall nowadays."

"And you think that's because I'm losing strength? Becoming weaker?" asked Stick Cat. You might think he would be offended by such a suggestion, but he wasn't. He appeared more amused than anything. There was just the hint of a grin on his face. "The fact that it's becoming harder and harder to pull you from the wall couldn't be for any other reason?"

"Not that comes to my mind, no," Edith replied. She lifted her paws in the air again and thrust them in Stick Cat's direction.

As he grasped her, Stick Cat added, "Maybe I'll start doing some push-ups or jumping jacks in the morning."

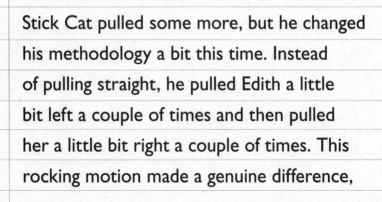

"Couldn't hurt," Edith said, and smiled. She seemed pleased that Stick Cat might heed her advice.

Stick Cat pulled some more, but he changed his methodology a bit this time. Instead of pulling straight, he pulled Edith a little bit left a couple of times and then pulled her a little bit right a couple of times. This rocking motion made a genuine difference, and in several seconds Edith's hips cleared the wall—and she popped free.

She paced across the bathroom floor, checked her fur in the mirror on the back of the door, and then turned her head over her shoulder. "Do you want to sit on the windowsill for a while?" she asked. "That wore me out. I need a rest."

Stick Cat smiled at her. "Great idea," he said.

It was a normal start to their day together.

But it was definitely *not* going to be a normal day.

Chapter 3

NO MORE RESCUES

After a long and glorious nap, Stick Cat and Edith woke up. Actually, Stick Cat woke up first, but he waited silently and motionlessly until Edith awakened too.

"What do you want to do today?" Stick Cat asked her.

"What time is it?"

Stick Cat looked out the window. He couldn't see the sun—there were too many buildings blocking his view—but he could discern where it was by the brightness of the sky.

"It's early afternoon, I think," Stick Cat answered. "That was a very long nap."

"I could sleep longer," Edith said. "I LOVE sleeping. I'd sleep right through the whole day if Tiffany didn't wake me up every morning."

"You would?"

"Most definitely," Edith said. She was quite sure of herself. "But she's always getting up and making my breakfast. She tries to be quiet, but she can't be. It drives me crazy! Then the smells from the kitchen come pouring into the room, and that wakes me up even more."

"What did she make for you this morning?"

"Huevos rancheros."

"What's that?"

"Scrambled eggs with
hot sauce," Edith answered.
She licked her lips in an
attempt to recapture
the flavors. "I LOVE hot sauce."

"I know you do. You're spicy."

"I'm TOTALLY spicy," Edith confirmed.
She liked being described this way, you
could tell. She licked her lips again—and it
seemed to remind her of something else.

"And bacon. I had seven strips of bacon. I'm in LOVE with bacon!"

Stick Cat smiled. "Sounds like it was a meal worth getting up for."

"I suppose," answered Edith casually. "I've had better."

Changing the subject, Stick Cat asked again, "What would you like to do today?"

Edith glanced out the window and up at the sky. Finally, an idea came to her. "We could take another nap. That would be fun."

"What about something a little more exciting?"

"Naps can be exciting."

"What about something a little more active?"

Edith didn't seem to like that idea too much. She rolled her eyes up and away from Stick Cat. She suddenly seemed quite determined about something.

"Let me tell you what we're *not* going to do today, Mr. Man," Edith stated. "We are *not* going to rescue some poor person who is stuck in a piano or is drowning in a massive pot of bagel batter."

"We're not?"

"No," Edith said, and shook her head. "I'm sick and tired of all these rescue missions. These people need to learn to take better care of themselves."

Now, Stick Cat did not agree with this attitude. But he also knew there was an incredibly small chance they would see another person who needed their help. And he certainly didn't think it would happen in the next few hours.

So he answered, "Okay."

"No more parachuting across the alley," Edith went on. "Even though it was tons of fun. I want today to be a rest day. A plain, simple, quiet rest day."

Again, Stick Cat said, "Okay."

And Edith closed her eyes again.

For fifteen seconds.

Cr-eea-k. Oomph!

"What was that?!" she screamed as her eyes snapped open.

Stick Cat leaped from the windowsill down to the living-room floor. He jerked and twitched his head left and right. He tried to identify the source of the sound.

"I think it came from the ceiling!" he whispered.

He was right. The sound did come from the ceiling. And he was right about something else too.

He and Edith would not try to rescue
someone today.

No.

Today they would try to *catch* someone.

Chapter 4

AN ELEPHANT IN THE CEILING

Edith was fully alert now. All her drowsiness had disappeared as soon as she heard that strange sound from the ceiling. She leaped down from the windowsill.

Cree-eeeak!

"There it is again!" she whispered. "What could it be?!"

Stick Cat had no idea. He had never heard such a strange sound before—and certainly never twice in a row. And definitely never from the ceiling.

Cree-eeeak!

Three times in a row.

"It's the ceiling!" exclaimed Edith. "It's going to collapse! There must be an elephant up there or something."

She took a few quiet steps to follow the sound. It was definitely moving —whatever it was.

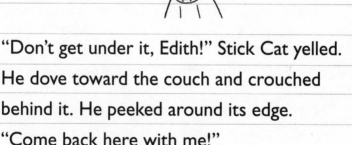

"Don't get under it, Edith!" Stick Cat yelled. He dove toward the couch and crouched behind it. He peeked around its edge. "Come back here with me!"

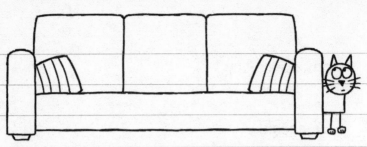

Edith continued to walk along with the sound. It was as if something was pushing through something else. There was a swishing sound now too—like a dragging sound.

"How do you think it got up there?" asked Edith.

"How do I think *what* got up there?"

"The elephant, of course!"

Cree-ee—eeak!

"Edith, an elephant is not in the ceiling."

"How do you know? It could be an elephant. You just won't admit that I'm right—that I figured it out first. That's what I think."

Stick Cat couldn't believe they were even having this discussion. He asked incredulously, "How could an elephant get in the ceiling?"

"That's what I just asked," Edith said. "That's what I want to know too."

Stick Cat could not be certain, but the ceiling seemed to bulge a bit with the sound—as if something heavy was slowly moving across the room right above them. It was an almost impossible thing to detect.

Precisely when Stick Cat wondered if he could indeed see a slight bulge moving across the ceiling, something happened.

And then something else happened.

Cra-aaa-ack!

CRACK!

A single piece of white plaster—about the size of a quarter—fell to the floor. And a thin crack shot out from that spot and ran in a jagged line across the ceiling.

"Edith!" Stick Cat screamed. "Get over here! Please! NOW!"

Edith stood directly under that bulgy spot—and didn't move an inch. Her chin was pointed up, her head twitched in tiny degrees as she followed that crack—and listened to that sound.

"It will be neat to see an elephant!" Edith said. "Imagine, just imagine, an elephant right here in our very own building."

"It's not an elephant!" Stick Cat repeated in a whisper-yell.

Edith didn't hear him—or, at least, wasn't paying particular attention to him anyway.

"You'd think we would have heard it stomping around," Edith continued. "I mean, elephants weigh at least eighty or ninety pounds. They're huge! And they blow those trunks like trumpets. You'd think we would have heard that once or twice."

"It's not an elephant," Stick Cat said again. He watched the crack move farther along the ceiling. It was almost to the wall now—almost to the big vent that blew cool air in the summer. Stick Cat stared at the large rectangular grate covering the vent. He tilted his head a bit to the side. It looked like he was trying to solve a puzzle.

Edith chatted away.

"No matter," she said, as much to herself as to anybody else. "We're going to see that elephant in no time."

"The vent," Stick Cat whispered. "Whatever it is will come out of the vent."

He bounded out from behind the couch, grasped Edith's front left paw, and began to pull her back to the couch.

"What the—?" Edith said, and resisted his efforts.

"Come on!"

"Why?"

"Something is going to come out of the vent in a few seconds!"

"I know that, silly," Edith said. "It's an elephant. I don't know how it's going to fit through that vent though."

Stick Cat continued to pull.

Edith continued to resist.

"If it's an elephant," Stick Cat said. It sounded like he was negotiating now in an attempt to change Edith's mind—and stop her from resisting. "Then I promise we'll come out to see it. We'll introduce ourselves. Become friends. Fix it a snack. Whatever."

"'Fix it a snack?'"

"Sure. If it's hungry," Stick Cat said, and yanked at Edith some more. He couldn't believe they were even talking about this. Something was crawling through the air-conditioning pipes toward the vent. It was not normal. Something extremely strange—probably even dangerous, Stick Cat thought—was happening. And here he was talking with Edith about fixing a snack for an elephant.

"I'm not sharing any of my food with an elephant," Edith huffed. "Forget it. I'm willing to be friends and all, but let's try to stay serious here."

Stick Cat had successfully pulled her back to the couch, at least. He took a little comfort in that. He thought they would be safer there. They peeked out from the back corner of the couch.

"Let's watch," Stick Cat whispered.

"How do you address an elephant?" Edith wondered out loud. "Is it like, 'Hey, Mr. Elephant'? Or is it more formal like, 'Good afternoon, Sir Elephant'? Or is it more like,

'Elephant. Dude. 'Sup?'"

GOOD AFTERNOON, SIR ELEPHANT.

"We're about to find out," Stick Cat said.

The air-conditioning vent shook. It rattled. Paint chips fell down from its edges onto the living-room carpet. Then the vent cover itself separated from the wall and dropped to the living-room carpet with a dull *THUD*!

Stick Cat and Edith stood perfectly still.

A long, thick, gray object fell out of the vent opening.

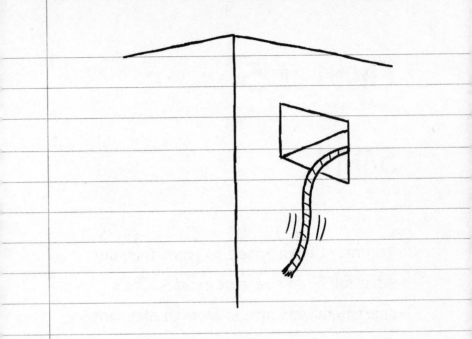

"Told you!" Edith exclaimed. "It's an elephant's trunk!"

Chapter 5

SANTA

You may be surprised to learn this, but what fell from the vent in Stick Cat's apartment was not, in fact, an elephant's trunk.

It was a rope. A long, thick, gray rope. It uncoiled and flopped and settled to the floor.

Edith asked, "Why would an elephant carry a rope with it?"

"Umm, I don't—" Stick Cat began to say.

"It's tough being right all the time," Edith interrupted. She was, apparently, still convinced there was an elephant up there. "But I don't understand why it would drag a rope with it."

"Umm—"

"Maybe it likes to play jump rope," Edith said quickly, coming up with her own theory before Stick Cat could even answer. "You know, to stay in shape."

Stick Cat tried to think of a response. "Umm."

Something happened just then that would disprove Edith's elephant theory.

A pair of shoes emerged from the vent—and a pair of pants after that.

"It's a person," Stick Cat whispered.

"It's probably the elephant trainer," Edith whispered back.

Despite being so curious—and so alarmed—about what was occurring, Stick Cat had to turn to Edith to see if she was, indeed, serious.

She was.

Edith saw the doubt on Stick Cat's face. As further explanation, she added, "The trainer probably uses the rope as a leash. You know, when the elephant isn't playing jump rope, I mean."

"Maybe so," Stick Cat said slowly. "But I think it might just be a man with a rope. And, you know, no elephant at all."

"So, you're saying a rope, but no elephant?"

"I think so."

"So, I'm half right," Edith said. She seemed to take some comfort in this idea. "Right about the rope, but possibly wrong about the elephant."

"Half right?" Stick Cat asked. "Uh, sure."

"Well, half right is better than half wrong."

Despite the danger of his home being invaded, Stick Cat had to smile. Only Edith, he figured, could think of her theory in this way. He said, "Yes. It is."

When Stick Cat turned back, a full-grown man had emerged from the vent. He leaned back, allowed the rope to support his weight, and stepped slowly down the wall. It took less than fifteen seconds for him to reach the floor.

He looked quite normal to Stick Cat—except for two

things. First, he wore a black
mask that covered his eyes and
the bridge of his nose. Second,
a leather satchel hung from his belt.

The masked man turned his
head slowly left and right,
examining the room quickly.

The man reached into his shirt pocket and
pulled out a second bag. This one was much
smaller and made of plastic. He crouched
down into a squatting position and then said
an astonishing thing. It was astonishing to
Stick Cat anyway.

"Here, kitty, kitty," he called. "Here, kitty.
I know you're in here. I heard you from
the vent. I think there might even be two
of you."

Edith began to step out from behind the couch, but Stick Cat stopped her.

"No, Edith," was all he said.

"Why not?"

"Are you serious? He snuck into my house!" answered Stick Cat.

"You have trust issues, Stick Cat," Edith said.

Stick Cat was about to say something, but the man did something before he could speak. He opened the plastic bag—and a scent flowed from it into the room.

"I have treats for you," the man called.

"He has treats, Stick Cat!" Edith said. "Can

you smell that? It smells like fish. Let's go get some!"

"No," answered Stick Cat simply.

The man took something from the bag. He pinched it between his pointer finger and thumb and held it suspended in the air in front of him.

He looked in their direction now. "I heard you meowing. I always carry something special with me just in case I meet a cute little kitty," he said, and pushed his hand in their direction. "It's tuna!"

"He thinks I'm cute!" Edith exclaimed. "And he has tuna! I LOVE tuna! Come on, let's go!"

"No, Edith."

Edith was frustrated. She pushed her lips together and squinted her eyes. She sniffed the air a bit. The tuna aroma continued to waft her way.

"Maybe he's *supposed* to be here, Stick Cat," she said. "Have you ever thought of that?"

"No, I haven't."

"Well, maybe he's a special cat-loving visitor. Maybe he visits cats all over the world—and brings them treats. And today it's our turn."

"Seriously?" Stick Cat asked. "You really think that?"

"It's possible," Edith said immediately. "Let's

go get some tuna and find out."

Stick Cat shook his head. "If he's so special,
then why did he sneak in here through the
air-conditioning vent?"

Edith contemplated this for a moment.
During that moment, the aroma of tuna
filled the room even more. This seemed to
encourage Edith to come up with a logical
explanation.

"Maybe he's like Santa Claus," Edith said,
and opened her eyes wide. "That explains it!
Like Santa Claus comes through chimneys,
this guy comes through air-conditioning
vents!"

"I don't think so."

"And he has a costume—just like Santa," Edith added. Now that she had come up with a theory, she believed in it wholeheartedly. "See the mask? That's his costume. What do you say we get some tuna? Hunh? Hunh?"

"I think it's more like a disguise than a costume."

"Costume, disguise, whatever," Edith said. She nudged her way past Stick Cat a bit. "Let's discuss this over a tuna snack. What do you say?"

"You really think this man is Santa Claus?"

"Well, not Santa specifically," Edith said. She seemed to be pleading her case. She really, really, really wanted some tuna—that was totally obvious. "He probably has a different name."

"Like what?" Stick Cat asked.

"I don't know," Edith said. All of Stick Cat's questions were bugging her. "Maybe it's Todd."

"Todd?"

"Sure, why not? Todd. Tuna Todd."

"So, let me get this straight," Stick Cat said. "You think 'Todd'—"

HELLO MY NAME IS
TUNA
TODD

"Tuna Todd," Edith corrected.

"Right, yeah. Tuna Todd," Stick Cat said, and continued. "You think Tuna Todd here is a hero of sorts. A guy who climbs through pipes all over the big city to pass out treats to cats?"

"A hero of some sort, that's for sure," Edith said, and nodded. "Sounds even more plausible when you add it all up, doesn't it?"

"No."

"Maybe a little tuna snack would help you get your mind around the idea."

"No," Stick Cat declared. "We stay put. Right here."

The masked man stood up—but not before placing the little chunk of tuna on a corner of the vent grate lying on the carpet.

"Suit yourself, little kitties," he said. "I can see you both back there. I'll leave this here for now. I'm just going to have a quick look around."

The masked man then opened the drawer of a table against the wall. Stick Cat knew exactly what was in there. It was one of his favorite playthings.

And Tuna Todd was going to take it.

Chapter 6

TUNA TODD GOES TO WORK

"A-ha!" exclaimed the man. There was pure delight in his voice. "A great find!"

He pulled a silver pocket watch from the drawer, swung it carefully on its chain for a moment. Its shiny surface glistened and sparkled as it reflected sunlight from the window. "This looks valuable."

Stick Cat watched the masked man quickly untie the leather satchel from his belt. He opened it and dropped the pocket watch inside.

Goose's grandfather had given the pocket watch to him on his tenth birthday. Goose had told the story as he swung the watch in the air and Stick Cat batted at it when he was a kitten.

And now it was gone.

"Do you still think this man—" Stick Cat began to ask Edith. But he was interrupted by her.

"His name is Tuna Todd," she said. "Remember?"

Stick Cat paused for three seconds, decided debating the man's name was not worth the time or effort, and asked Edith the whole question this time.

"Do you still think Tuna Todd is a hero?"

"Sure," Edith answered quickly. "Why wouldn't I?"

"He just stole Goose's watch!"

"That was a watch?"

"Yes," sighed Stick Cat. "Goose's grandpa gave it to him."

This took Edith aback. You could tell it bothered her. She cast her eyes down to the floor and shook her head slightly. She looked upset.

But only for six seconds.

After that short period of time, she lifted her head. Her expression had changed. She was smiling now.

"It makes perfect sense," she said. "Of course he took it."

"What?!" Stick Cat asked in complete disbelief. "How does that make sense?!"

"Think about it, Stick Cat," Edith explained. "Tuna Todd makes dozens—maybe hundreds—of delicious fishy deliveries every day. He brings joy to cats all over the world. Now, to do that he needs to stay on a pretty tight schedule, don't you think? A watch is vital for Tuna Todd to do his job."

Stick Cat said nothing. There was a reason for that: he could think of nothing to say.

After rummaging through the drawer a little more, the man walked quietly to the kitchen. He seemed to have already forgotten about the cats. He concentrated fully on his task.

Stick Cat followed him. Edith left their spot behind the couch as well. But she took a little detour before joining Stick Cat at the kitchen doorway. When she did eventually stand next to him, Edith licked her whiskers and smacked her lips a couple of times.

Stick Cat couldn't resist. He had to ask.

"How was the tuna?"

"Excuse me?" Edith answered. She did her best to look surprised.

"The tuna?" repeated Stick Cat. "You stopped to eat the tuna on the way over here, didn't you?"

"Excuse me?"

Stick Cat pointed toward the air-conditioning vent cover on the floor. There was clearly no longer any tuna on it. "The tuna?"

Edith glanced back over her shoulder, realized

there was likely no other explanation, and decided to admit what she had done. But she did so in typical Edith fashion.

"Stick Cat," she began to explain. "That tuna was absolutely delicious! I'm so happy that Tuna Todd leaves it for deserving, well-behaved, good-looking cats all over the world."

Stick Cat smiled, nodded, and commented, "You certainly are all of those things."

"You're right about that," Edith said. She then asked, "What's Tuna Todd up to now?"

Stick Cat turned his attention back toward the masked man in the kitchen. He was opening and closing drawers. He didn't seem very satisfied with his findings. He

kept whispering things like, "Nothing here"
and "Zero" and "Where's the good stuff?"

Finally he reached for the cookie jar on the
counter next to the sink.
The jar, like many other
things in Stick Cat's home,
had a picture of a goose
on it.

Stick Cat knew exactly what was in that jar—
and he knew the masked man would take it.

For years, Goose had put paper money into
that jar every week. Goose liked to call it his
"Paris, France jar."

You see, Paris was the one place in the
whole world where Goose wanted to travel

the most. Sometimes, he would talk to Stick Cat about it. Goose said he would

eat out at fancy restaurants, climb the Eiffel Tower, and eat grapes right off the vine for breakfast.

Stick Cat could tell it was the one thing that Goose always wanted to do the most.

But Goose hadn't made that trip yet for one simple reason. He wanted to take someone with him—someone really special who he hadn't met yet.

So, on Sunday night every week, Goose got his wallet, pulled some money out, and stuffed it into the jar on the counter. If Stick

Cat was close, Goose would look at him and say, "One day, little buddy, I'll find the right girl and the three of us will all go to Paris."

Then he'd scratch Stick Cat under the chin and wash the dishes.

For Stick Cat, it was kind of nice and sad all rolled up together. It was fun to listen to Goose talk about his dream, but it was sad he hadn't met someone to share it with.

And now Goose would never get the opportunity. Because the masked man reached into the cookie jar and said one thing with pure delight.

"Jackpot!"

He took all the money out, stuffed it into

his satchel, and smiled the meanest, nastiest smile Stick Cat had ever seen.

Stick Cat was angry.

Really angry.

Stick Cat took two steps into the kitchen and snarled at the man.

The burglar turned to him, but he clearly misinterpreted Stick Cat's intention.

"Well, look who's back," the man said. He looked past Stick Cat and Edith into the living room and saw that the tuna was no longer on the vent cover. "Came back for a little more tuna, right?"

As soon as he said this, Edith stepped into

the kitchen and joined Stick Cat.

"All right," the man said. He took the plastic bag from his pocket and placed two more big pinches of tuna on the floor. "Here you go, kitties. After that cookie jar find, I'm in a very, very good mood! Let's see if I have any luck in the bedroom, shall we?"

The masked man stepped through the doorway—Stick Cat actually needed to dodge out of his way to avoid being stomped on. The man headed straight to Goose and Stick Cat's bedroom.

Stick Cat stood perfectly still.

He had never felt this mad before. He had been scared before. He'd crossed the alley twice, after all. One time, he and Edith had used an apron on a clothesline twenty-three floors above street level. Another time they used a black cable and a napkin as a sort of zip line to get across.

Yes, he had been plenty frightened both those times—scared out of his wits actually.

But this was different.

He wasn't frightened.

He was angry.

He made a decision right then and right there.

He would try to stop this thief.

He didn't know how.

And he didn't think he stood a chance.

But that didn't mean Stick Cat wouldn't try.

And he knew he'd need help.

"Edith," he said. "I'm going to try—"

But Edith was no longer there.

Chapter 7

IT EVAPORATED

Edith was eating the tuna.

"Edith!" Stick Cat yelled.

She didn't look up. Edith kept her full attention on the two little mounds of tuna.

Well, it was actually just one little mound of tuna. She had already consumed the first one.

"Edith!"

She still didn't look up.

Stick Cat watched as the masked man disappeared into the bedroom.

"Edith!"

Finally, she lifted her head.

The tuna was gone.

"I'm sorry, Stick Cat," she replied. She licked some tuna bits from her lips. "I didn't hear you calling. I must have been busy with something else."

Despite the fact that he was anxious and nervous and worried about what was happening inside his apartment, Stick Cat had to smile. "No problem," he said. "How was the tuna this time?"

Edith licked her lips again.
"Even better than the first
time! I swear!"

"Maybe I should try a taste,"
Stick Cat suggested.

"Umm, it's a good idea
and everything," responded Edith.
"But, umm, there's none left."

"None?"

"None."

"Where did it all go?" asked Stick Cat. There
was just a hint of mischief in his voice, but
Edith didn't seem to notice at all. She seemed

mostly preoccupied with licking the final tasty tuna morsels from her whiskers. "I thought there were two portions."

"Yes, there were, Stick Cat," Edith said quickly, and nodded. "Yes, there were. That's very observant of you. Way to pay attention to every detail."

"Where did the other portion go?"

"Excuse me?"

"I asked, 'Where did the other portion go?'"

"Oh, well, that's a very good question," Edith said, and shifted her eyes away from Stick Cat. "A very good question indeed."

Stick Cat knew Edith was stalling for time to

think of a way to respond. He asked, "But do you have a very good answer?"

"I do. Yes."

"Okay, then. What happened to that second portion of tuna?"

Edith remained turned away from Stick Cat—but only for eight seconds. Her shoulders twitched a little. It was a slight—almost imperceptible—grin that came to her face. She turned to Stick Cat then. With utter confidence, she said just two words.

EVAPORATING TUNA

"It evaporated."

"It evaporated?"

"It evaporated."

"My portion of tuna evaporated?" Stick Cat asked again. "Is that what you're saying?"

"That's what I'm saying," answered Edith. She was ready to move on. "I'm glad we cleared that up."

"I thought only liquids could evaporate," Stick Cat said. Now, truthfully, Stick Cat had no intention of eating a portion of tuna anyway. There was no way he would take anything from this man who stole from Goose. It wouldn't be right. But the idea of having a bit of fun with Edith during this tense time seemed like a good one. "I didn't think solids could evaporate."

"Lots of things can evaporate," Edith said, defending her position.

"Like what?"

"Water, for instance."

"It does. But that's a liquid," said Stick Cat. "Tuna is a solid."

Edith clearly didn't want to continue this conversation, but she didn't quite know how to end it. "What *is* tuna, Stick Cat?"

"It's a fish."

"Exactly," Edith said. "It's a fish. There's your explanation."

Stick Cat shook his head. "What?"

"Fish swim, right?" Edith asked. She was already growing impatient.

"Right."

"Where do they swim?"

"In the ocean."

"What's the ocean made of?"

"Water."

"And water *evaporates*, Stick Cat," Edith said. There was a hint of triumph in her voice.

"But—"

"No buts," Edith said, and shook her head.

"But just because tuna swim in water and water evaporates, that doesn't mean—" Stick Cat began to say, but he was interrupted.

"It's all *connected*, Stick Cat. It's all *connected*!"

Stick Cat could think of nothing at all to say.

Having concluded her side of the conversation to her satisfaction, Edith looked around the room and asked, "Where did Tuna Todd go?"

"To the bedroom," answered Stick Cat.

As soon as Stick Cat answered, Edith hustled off in that direction.

"Where are you going?"

"To the bedroom, of course," Edith called over her shoulder. "To help Tuna Todd."

"To HELP him?!"

"Absolutely," Edith answered without hesitation. "I love this guy."

"He's stealing, Edith! He's not even allowed to be here."

"And I suppose Santa isn't allowed into homes either."

"This guy is NOT Santa."

"He's *like* Santa," Edith said. As she hurried to the bedroom, she made one last comment. "And that's good enough for me."

Stick Cat did not hurry off. He waited. He wasn't altogether sure he wanted to watch the masked burglar anymore. There was nothing he could do to stop him. Tuna Todd was just too big.

But Stick Cat wasn't going to give up just yet.

He was determined to find some way—any way—to stop the man.

He headed to the bedroom.

When he got there, Stick Cat couldn't
believe what he saw.

Chapter 8

MAGIC TUNA DUST

Edith was on Goose's bed.

She sat back on her rear legs and held her front paws up in front of herself in an obvious begging position.

Tuna Todd stood before her. He tore little chunks of tuna off a bigger piece and dropped them into Edith's mouth.

He asked, "Who's a good kitty?"

"I am!" Edith exclaimed. Of course, Tuna
Todd couldn't understand what she said—
but he encouraged her just the same.

"Who wants some more tuna?" he asked,
and held another piece of fish in front of her.

"I do, Tuna Todd!" Edith screamed. She was
springing up and down on her back legs now.
"I do!"

"You're not going to tell anybody I was here,
are you?"

"No, Tuna Todd! Never!" exclaimed Edith.
She stretched up and forward and snatched
the tuna from the burglar's hand. "Your
secret identity is safe with me, Tuna Todd!"

"Edith!" screamed Stick Cat from the

doorway. "What are you doing?!"

She was far too busy chewing to answer, but the man turned his head quickly upon hearing Stick Cat.

"Ahh, you want your share too, hunh?" the burglar said upon spotting Stick Cat. He had obviously misinterpreted Stick Cat's sounds again. He yanked off another chunk of tuna and tossed it toward Stick Cat. "Here you go, kitty."

Now, Stick Cat had absolutely no intention of eating that tuna from this terrible man. He looked forward to turning his head away from that chunk of fish—or maybe even batting it back at him. That would teach this mean burglar a lesson.

But Stick Cat never even got the chance.

That's because as soon as that tuna was airborne—as soon as it began traveling in a graceful arc toward Stick Cat—something happened.

Do you know what happened?

I bet you do.

I'll tell you in case you don't.

Edith sprang from the bed and snatched that tuna from the air before it even began its descent.

She snared the flying tuna chunk in her teeth

85

and landed gracefully on all fours on the bedroom carpet. She had already swallowed it when the burglar spoke.

"Wow!" he exclaimed. "That's the way I do things too! Take whatever I want, whenever I want. You are my kind of cat!"

"And you are my kind of cat-loving superhero!" Edith exclaimed with true admiration.

"Edith!"

She turned a guilty head over her shoulder as her tongue circled her lips in search of extra tuna bits.

"Yes, Stick Cat?"

"How can you do that?"

"How can I do what?"

"Play with this terrible person?"

"I like to play."

"And how can you eat treats from him?!"

"The eating is the best part," Edith explained casually. In truth, she seemed slightly relieved that Stick Cat wasn't upset about her snatching his tuna portion out of midair. She continued, "But you have to eat it correctly."

Stick Cat was frustrated with Edith. That was certain. But he had to ask, "What do you mean? What's the right way to eat tuna?"

"I'm glad you asked," answered Edith. She was all too happy to explain. "You see, I have a very sophisticated palate. It's taken me years to refine my tasting capabilities. My taste buds have not been dulled and sullied by pouch food. No. My taste buds have been developed and nurtured by my love of finer, more elegant cuisine. I'm quite a conundrum."

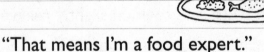

"Conundrum?"

"That means I'm a food expert."

"I think you mean connoisseur."

Edith didn't like being corrected—or interrupted. You could tell. She hesitated a few seconds, closed her eyes very slowly, and then opened them just as slowly.

"As I was saying," Edith continued. "To eat and savor tuna properly, you must hold it in your mouth for a moment. You must let that awesome tuna goodness spread all around. You must combine the tuna with the liquid in your mouth. You must let it swim. It must swim, Stick Cat! It must swim!!"

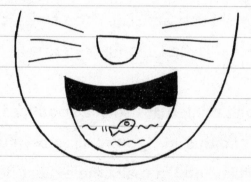

Stick Cat had never seen Edith quite this worked up. She was delighting in her description.

"After the tuna, umm, swims," said Stick Cat. "Then what do you do?"

Edith nodded at the question. She appreciated that Stick Cat recognized her expertise.

"Then," Edith said, and paused. "Then you just chew it and swallow it as fast as you can! I'm REALLY good at eating fast!"

"Wow," Stick Cat said. "You make it sound so nice. Maybe I should try some."

"I don't think that's such a good idea, Stick Cat," Edith said. "You've already refused it twice. And I'm really the expert here. When Tuna Todd sprinkles the world with Magic Tuna Dust, you should just let me take care of it."

"'Magic Tuna Dust'?"

"That's right," Edith said. "That's how
I've come to think of his tasty tuna
distributions—Magic Tuna Dust."

Stick Cat hung his head.

He truly didn't know what to do. He knew
it would be hard to convince Edith this man
was a bad person when she thought he was
some kind of hero spreading *Magic Tuna Dust*
all over the place.

What Stick Cat did not know was this: the
burglar himself would soon convince Edith
that he needed to be stopped.

Chapter 9

SOCK BALLS

Stick Cat watched as the man pulled out every drawer in Goose's dresser.

"Sometimes, the really good stuff is hidden under the clothes," the man said to himself. He seemed so wrapped up in what he was doing that he had forgotten entirely about Stick Cat and Edith. He dug his hands into all the drawers, pushing through Goose's T-shirts, pants, and boxer shorts without finding anything. The last drawer contained all of Goose's socks. They were rolled up into balls.

"Ahh, the sock drawer," the man said with a sense of anticipation. "I've found some of my finest treasures in the sock drawer."

His back was turned toward Stick Cat and Edith as he sifted through Goose's rolled-up socks.

The man huffed a bit to himself and said, "Too many. I can't find anything in here."

And with that, the man began to fling Goose's socks over his shoulder. The sock balls rained down from the air all around Edith and Stick Cat. The socks bounced on the bed and fell to the floor. They bounced on the carpet and rolled to a stop.

It was too much for Edith to resist.

She leaped into the air and bounded after the sock balls as they fell from the air, tumbled off the bed, and rolled across the carpet.

"Come on, Stick Cat!" Edith squealed as she bounced about to bat the bouncing balls. "It's totally fun! Tuna Todd wants to play!"

"He's not playing, Edith!" Stick Cat sighed. He was clearly tired of trying to convince Edith that Tuna Todd was a bad person. "He's just trying to steal more things."

"Whee!" Edith mewed with delight as the burglar tossed more and more sock balls over his shoulder. "Here come some more!"

It only took about twenty seconds before the man emptied the sock drawer entirely. He had found nothing else to steal.

"Nothing," the man said to himself, and checked his watch. "I should be going anyway. Been here long enough."

The burglar then stepped around Edith, Stick Cat, and all the scattered sock balls on the way to the living room. He continued to speak to himself as he walked.

"Not too bad," the burglar said as he reached for the rope and pulled it taut. He tugged at it a few times to ensure it was secure and would hold his weight. He seemed confident that it would—and he seemed satisfied with his visit to Goose and Stick Cat's apartment. "A pretty good haul, I'd say. A silver pocket watch and a bunch of cash. Let's see what I can get at the next stop."

And with that the man climbed the rope and disappeared through the air-conditioning vent.

"Good-bye, Tuna Todd!" Edith called with delight. "Thanks for the Magic Tuna Dust! And the sock ball game! It was totally fun!"

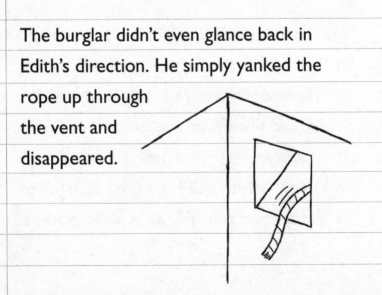

The burglar didn't even glance back in Edith's direction. He simply yanked the rope up through the vent and disappeared.

But Edith wasn't offended. As if providing an explanation for her hero's hasty departure, Edith said, "He has to hurry off to the next cat household. You know, to spread more joy and cheer to other kitties throughout the world. I totally understand."

Stick Cat could not respond. He dropped his head and stared at the floor. He was sad and angry about what had just happened—and bewildered by Edith's misinterpretation of it.

"Come back soon, Tuna Todd," Edith called up to the now-empty vent. "And don't forget your Magic Tuna Dust!"

Stick Cat raised his head, glanced back and forth a couple of times between the vent and Edith. He whispered, "Oh, for the love

of—" But he didn't say anything else—
because Edith interrupted him.

"Hey, Stick Cat?"

"Yes?"

"How about another nap? My tummy's full,
and I'm tired from all that sock play."

Stick Cat was tired too—exhausted really.
Witnessing this burglar commit those crimes
and his inability to do anything about it was
so frustrating—and so tiring.

"Fine," he said.

But Edith didn't hear him.

She was already asleep.

Stick Cat closed his eyes. He wanted to sleep too. He wanted to forget what had just happened—even for just a little while.

He concentrated on the pattern of Edith's snoring.

Haunk-shoo. Haunk-shoo. Haunk-shoo.

He concentrated on that rhythm—and waited for sleep to come.

Haunk-shoo. Haunk-shoo.

He waited. And listened.

Haunk-shoo.

Until another sound interrupted everything.

THUD!

And then
the floor shook.

THUD!

Chapter 10

IT'S THE TOILET

"Edith!"

Edith opened one eye halfway to acknowledge Stick Cat, but she didn't say a word.

"Edith!" Stick Cat repeated. "Wake up! I heard something. I think it's coming from the bathroom!"

Edith yawned and closed that one eye again. She said, "Someone probably just flushed the toilet."

Now, even Stick Cat—who was perfectly familiar with Edith's odd answers and ideas—had to pause at this suggestion.

"There's nobody here," Stick Cat said.

"We're here," Edith whispered without opening her eyes.

"And we were both here in the living room," Stick Cat explained. "And I know what a toilet sounds like. And—"

But Stick Cat stopped himself.

Edith wasn't listening.

She was snoring again.

As Stick Cat shook his head, more strange

sounds came from the bathroom. It was as if the noise was distant—farther than the bathroom or something—but still coming from that direction.

"What is that?" Stick Cat whispered, and cocked his head to aim his left ear that way. It sounded like several things were opening and closing in succession.

And then Stick Cat's eyes flashed open wide.

He knew what it was.

He knew *who* it was.

"Edith!" he yelled.

"I told you," she said without moving a

whisker. "It's the toilet."

"I'm pretty sure it wasn't the toilet."

"Maybe it's another elephant," suggested Edith. "Since there wasn't one before, the odds are much better it's an elephant this time."

Stick Cat hung his head and stared at the thick, plush carpet beneath his front paws. He inhaled and exhaled three times in a row. In a much calmer voice, he said, "I think there's someone in your apartment, Edith."

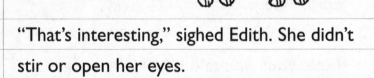

"That's interesting," sighed Edith. She didn't stir or open her eyes.

"I think all those strange sounds are coming through our hole in the bathroom cabinets," Stick Cat said. So far, he was keeping his composure. "Someone's in your apartment. And I think I know who it is."

Edith rolled her head a bit in an attempt to loosen her neck muscles and settle into a more comfortable resting position.

"It's probably Tiffany. She must have come home from work early or something," replied Edith. She shook her head ever so slightly. "This better not affect her paycheck. I found a single loose thread on my cashmere blanket. I need a new one."

Stick Cat ignored the whole cashmere blanket thing. He recognized an opportunity to get Edith up and on her feet.

"If it's Tiffany, then you have to get home right away!" exclaimed Stick Cat. "You can't get caught over here! Tiffany and Goose will find the hole. They'll plug it up! We won't be able to see each other anymore!"

Edith opened her eyes then.

But just barely.

She contemplated the whole situation—and considered her options.

"Let's see, let's see," she said, more to herself than to Stick Cat. "I could stay here. I have a belly full of tuna, I'm really sleepy, and this carpet is so soft and comfortable— but I might get busted by Tiffany."

Stick Cat inhaled and exhaled methodically

two more times as he waited.

"Or," Edith said. "I could get up and walk all that long, long, long way to the bathroom, probably get stuck in the wall, wait for you to push me through—all so we don't get into trouble."

Stick Cat continued to breathe slowly.

"It's a tough call," Edith said. "Nap or get caught. Nap or get caught."

Edith rested her chin on her front paws.

And closed her eyes.

She had apparently chosen the nap option.

Stick Cat shook his head. He was out of ideas.

Thankfully, he didn't need to come up with another idea to get Edith alert and moving. Because at precisely that moment a loud clanging noise boomed out from the bathroom.

"Oh, for criminy's sake!" Edith huffed. She opened her eyes and shook her head back and forth quickly four times. "How am I supposed to sleep with all that racket?! What is Tiffany doing in there?!"

CLANG!

"I don't think it's Tiffany," responded Stick Cat.

"Well, who else could it be?" Edith asked, and stood up. She seemed unfortunately resigned to the fact that she would need to move. "I'm the only other one who lives there, Stick Cat. And, I don't know if you've noticed or not, but I'm right here in front of you. Helll-looo."

"I don't think it's Tiffany," Stick Cat repeated. "And I don't think it's you."

"Well," Edith said, and arched her back, stretching the sleepiness from her body. "Who is it then, Mr. Smarty-Pants?"

Stick Cat looked Edith directly in the eyes.

He said, "I think it's Tuna Todd."

"Tuna Todd?!"

"I think so," Stick Cat replied. "He's probably trying to st—"

"That's great!" Edith screamed, and hurried off to the bathroom. "I'm hungry again!"

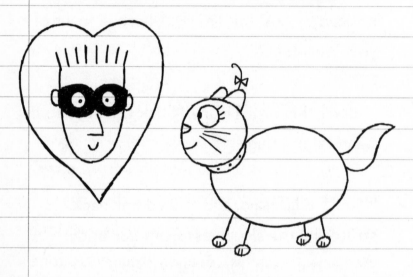

Chapter 11

ANOTHER JACKPOT

Stick Cat had never seen Edith move so quickly—and so soon—after a nap.

Typically after sleeping, Edith's eyes would open slowly. She would push her front paws forward and push her body up. Then she would stretch her rear legs straight back one at a time. Only after this two-minute routine would she take her first step after a nap.

That is not what happened this time.

As soon as Edith thought Tuna Todd might be in her apartment, she bolted across the living room in a straight line to the bathroom. Stick Cat hustled after her.

By the time he entered the bathroom, Edith had already dived into the cabinet and plunged into the hole between their apartments.

It was only then that she stopped moving quickly.

I bet you know why.

She was stuck.

"Stick Cat!" Edith called.

"I'm right here," Stick Cat replied, and ducked his head into the bathroom cabinet.

He saw exactly what he thought he would see—Edith's tail, back legs, and hindquarters.

"Well, hurry and give me a push," Edith pleaded. Stick Cat could hear her muffled words clearly enough. "He could be spreading Magic Tuna Dust all over the place and there's nobody there to eat it! This is an emergency!"

Stick Cat felt anxious. He was mad about the burglar taking the watch and money from Goose. He suspected this awful man was now going to steal things from Tiffany and Edith's apartment too. He didn't want to watch that.

But seeing Edith stuck in the wall for the umpteenth time and knowing her desire for more tuna drove all her actions was certainly amusing. He smiled a bit and shoved Edith the rest of the way through the hole—and Stick Cat followed after her.

He trailed Edith to the kitchen first. The room was in total disarray—drawers were open and emptied. Napkins, silverware, and papers were scattered all over the floor. The cabinets were all open.

"It's Tuna Todd, all right," Stick Cat said. "He was in here looking for more things to steal."

"Not necessarily," Edith said quickly in Tuna

Todd's defense. "Even if it is him, maybe he came in here to find something to eat."

"What?!"

"He's probably famished, Stick Cat," explained Edith. "Imagine, just imagine. He travels throughout the world sprinkling Magic Tuna Dust over all the good cats everywhere. I'm sure he works up quite an appetite. Did you ever think of that?"

"Umm, no," answered Stick Cat. He tried for a moment to think of something else to say, but he didn't need to. Because right then a man's voice called out from the bedroom.

It was Tuna Todd.

"Jackpot!"

"It's him!" Edith exclaimed. Then she turned to Stick Cat and asked, "Do you know what time it is?"

Stick Cat shook his head. You could tell he wasn't looking forward to the answer.

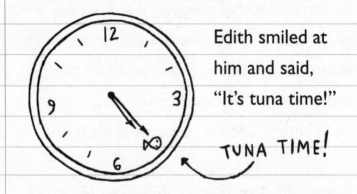

Edith smiled at him and said, "It's tuna time!"

TUNA TIME!

Then she bounded out of the kitchen, sprinted through the living room, and entered her and Tiffany's bedroom.

Stick Cat followed her. As he passed through the living room on the way to the bedroom, Stick Cat saw another vent cover on the floor. Tuna Todd had obviously come straight here from his and Goose's apartment.

The burglar was hunched over the bedroom dresser. His back was toward Stick Cat and Edith as they stood inside the doorway and observed him. His hands moved quickly and there was a distinct metallic clinking sound coming from his direction.

Leaning closer toward Edith, Stick Cat whispered, "What's on the dresser?"

"Just Tiffany's jewelry box," Edith whispered back. She then licked her lips and asked a question back. "Do you think Tuna Todd has any Magic Tuna Dust left?"

"Umm," Stick Cat said, and paused.

"And one other question."

"Yes?"

"Why are we whispering?"

"So he doesn't know we're here," Stick Cat answered, and paced a couple of quiet steps backward. He nodded toward Edith to follow him—and, thankfully, she did. Once they were positioned outside the bedroom doorway and just peeking into the room, Stick Cat continued with his explanation. "We don't want him to see us."

"Why not?" Edith asked, and cocked her head. "If he doesn't know we're here, then he won't sprinkle us with scrumptious

Magic Tuna Dust."

Stick Cat shook his head ever so slightly, but Edith didn't notice.

"We want to surprise him," Stick Cat whispered. He tried to think of something—anything—to stop this man.

"We do?"

"Yes," Stick Cat said.

While this conversation occurred, the burglar continued to empty all the individual drawers and trays in the jewelry box.

"Are we going to surprise him with a treat of his own?" Edith asked.

Stick Cat stopped observing the man stealing all of Tiffany's jewelry and turned to Edith. He asked, "Why in the world would we do that?"

"Well, it seems only fair," Edith said without hesitation. She had apparently thought this through a bit. "You know how kids leave cookies and milk for Santa?"

"Yes."

"I think we should do a similar thing for Tuna Todd," Edith explained. "We'll make him a snack. Maybe a ham-and-cheese sandwich. Or spaghetti and meatballs."

"Umm—"

"And you
know how
kids leave
the treats by the fireplace for Santa," Edith
whispered quickly. She seemed to get more
and more enamored with her idea as she
spoke about it. She really liked where this
was all going. "They do that because that's
where Santa gets in and out of each house."

"Umm—"

Edith didn't give Stick Cat any more time to
respond. She was pretty worked up.

"Well," she went on. "We'll leave the

sandwich or pasta for Tuna Todd near the air-conditioning vent. Since that's where *he* goes in and out."

Stick Cat just looked at Edith.

And looked at her some more.

He could think of nothing at all to say. He knew he would have to convince Edith that Tuna Todd was not a Santa-like person. He glanced toward the burglar, who had now turned a little sideways to make it easier to dump the contents of the jewelry box's largest drawer into his bag.

"Great idea, right?" Edith asked, and nodded her head with true enthusiasm.

"Look," Stick Cat whispered and pointed.

He and Edith watched
as Tiffany's glittering
necklaces and
sparkling bracelets
fell into the bag.

"That sure is sweet!"
Edith exclaimed quietly.

"What?!" Stick Cat whispered, and tugged
Edith backward—farther out of the
doorway. "Sweet?!"

"Oh, yes," Edith said. They were not
completely hidden from the burglar. "*Very*
sweet. Don't you see, Stick Cat? Tuna Todd
uses all that jewelry to make special presents
for good kitties. He uses the diamonds,
rubies, sapphires, and other gemstones to
create beaded collars, fancy ribbons, and

decorative food bowls for all the good kitties all over the world."

"You really believe that?!"

"Without a doubt," Edith said. "He's Tuna Todd. He takes from bad people and gives to good kitties."

"So, Tiffany is bad?"

"She's no great shakes," Edith said, and shrugged. "Just yesterday morning, for instance, my eggs Benedict were average at best. The hollandaise sauce wasn't rich enough. I think she used milk instead of cream. That really takes away from the overall flavor and complexity of the dish."

Stick Cat shook his head ever so slightly and then said, "You're saying it's okay if he steals from Tiffany."

"Oh, certainly," Edith answered.

"But she's your roommate."

"So?"

"She gives you silk pillows and cashmere blankets."

"What's your point?"

"She feeds you!"

"She's not that great a cook. Didn't you hear what I just said about the eggs Benedict?" Edith asked. That made her think of another meal. "And last night my trout amandine was slightly overdone. I like my fish a little more tender."

"So, it's okay if he steals things from people as long as he uses those things to then leave gifts for cats all over the world?"

"That's right," answered Edith. She seemed relieved that Stick Cat had begun to understand. "Now you're catching on. It took you long enough."

"Then why didn't he leave something for me? At my apartment?"

"I guess you weren't very good this year," Edith said matter-of-factly. "You must be on the naughty kitty list."

"And where does Tuna Todd do all this?" asked Stick Cat. Then he added, "Wait. Don't tell me. The North Pole, right?"

"Don't be ridiculous, Stick Cat," Edith sighed. "The North Pole is Santa's territory. That's where Santa's workshop is. You know, with the leprechauns and walruses."

"Do you mean elves and reindeer?"

"Whatever."

The whole conversation, of course, was entirely bizarre to Stick Cat. And Tuna Todd continued to rummage through Tiffany's belongings to try to find more things to steal. Stick Cat was frightened.

But he couldn't help himself.

He had to find out a few more details about Edith's Tuna Todd theory.

He asked, "Where's, umm, Tuna Todd's workshop then?"

"I'm not sure," Edith said. "Somewhere equally exotic and private, I would think. Philadelphia, Cleveland, Kilcrohane, Birmingham. Somewhere like that."

This conversation would have, no doubt, continued for some time.

But it stopped right there.

Tuna Todd said something at that exact moment that grabbed Edith's full attention.

"What's this?" he asked out loud. He had

by now emptied all the contents of Tiffany's jewelry box into his satchel and moved on to the dresser drawers. "Balls of yarn? Dozens of them. This looks like a good hiding place."

Edith immediately started into the bedroom, but Stick Cat stopped her after just two strides. He reached out and tugged gently on her collar.

"Where are you going?!" he asked in an urgent whisper.

"Tuna Todd is ready to play again! What a great guy! Balls of yarn are even more fun than sock balls. I LOVE to play with balls of yarn! I need to let him know I'm here!" Edith answered upon turning her head over her shoulder. When she did so, she noticed Stick Cat's paw on her collar. "And would you kindly remove your paw? Now."

Stick Cat withdrew his paw as fast as he could.

"Why does Tiffany have a whole drawer of yarn balls?" asked Stick Cat. It appeared as if he was trying to distract Edith—trying to delay her a bit.

"Oh, she's always knitting me stuff. Sweaters, booties, that kind of thing," answered Edith. "She worked for weeks on a set of pink booties for me last winter. She didn't want my paws to get cold."

"That was nice of her," Stick Cat responded genuinely. "I've never seen you wear any knitted things."

"I never wore them," explained Edith.

"Why?"

"They were cotton," Edith explained. "I won't wear something that common. Now, if they were knitted from angora, then I might consider trying them on at least. Maybe. But probably not."

"Why not?"

"Because she'd probably knit the booties in pink again."

"What's wrong with that?"

Edith shook her head. She couldn't believe that Stick Cat would ask such a ridiculous question. "Booties are autumn and winter apparel, Stick Cat. You only wear them when it's cold outside."

"Okay, but I still don't understand."

"Pink is a spring color," Edith sighed. "I'd never wear pink in winter. Tiffany has no fashion sense whatsoever."

"She worked for weeks on those booties and you refused to wear them because they were the wrong color for the season?"

"And they were made out of cotton. Don't forget that."

"Right," remembered Stick Cat. "And made

out of cotton."

"I'm glad you understand."

"Umm," Stick Cat said, and hesitated. He
knew he didn't have much time. Tuna Todd
had already emptied more than a dozen yarn
balls from the drawer. They were scattered
about on the floor. But he still had one more
question he wanted to ask Edith about the
booties. So he asked it. "How did you let
Tiffany know you
didn't like them?"

"Oh, that was easy."

"How'd you do it?"

"I dropped them
in the toilet."

"You dropped them in the toilet?!"

"Then I flushed them."

"You flushed them?!"

"I flushed them."

Now, this conversation might have continued for a little while longer.

But it didn't.

Do you want to guess why?

You don't have to guess. I'll just tell you.

At that precise moment, the burglar caught the glimmer of something glittery and sparkly from the corner of his eye.

And when Edith realized what the man had noticed her entire attitude changed drastically.

Chapter 12

BUT I'M A GOOD KITTY

"What do we have here?!" the man
said, and took his hands out of the yarn
drawer. He didn't even bother to close it.
Something else had caught his attention.
There was sheer glee in his voice. "My, my,
my! These look valuable!"

Tiffany and Edith's large queen-sized bed
was situated in the middle of the bedroom.
On the right side was one pillow and a
cotton blanket—that was Tiffany's side.
On the left side were three pillows—one
soft, one medium, and one hard—and a
cashmere blanket.

The left side was, obviously, Edith's side.

Tiffany had an alarm clock and a lamp on a small table by her side of the bed.

But that's not what the burglar noticed.

What the burglar noticed was next to the left side of the bed.

Edith's side of the bed.

Hanging on the wall there were Edith's collars. She had one for each day of the week. Each collar hung from a peg on a board attached to the wall. Only one collar was missing—the Tuesday collar.

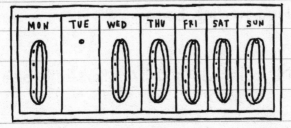

Today was Tuesday.

And that collar was around Edith's neck right now.

But soon the other six collars would be gone too.

The burglar took two quick, long strides to Edith's side of the bed and reached for a collar.

"What's he *doing?!*" a wide-eyed Edith asked Stick Cat in an angry whisper. She breathed fast, her shoulders were hunched a bit, and the fur on her back was up.

"He's stealing, Edith."

"My collars?! My daily collars?! My beautiful,

colorful collars?!"

"Yes."

"He's stealing from me?!"

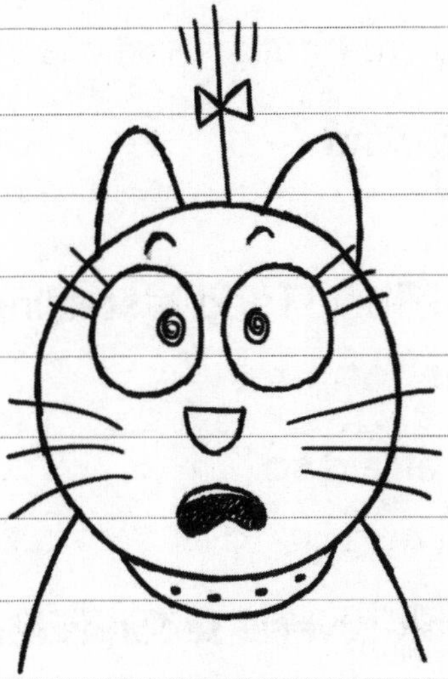

"Yes."

"A cat?!"

"That's right."

"But I'm a good kitty."

"I know you are."

"I'm a great kitty!"

"I know."

"I'm a fabulous, beautiful, and totally modest kitty!"

"Mm-hmm."

"And Tuna Todd is stealing from me?"

"I'm afraid so."

It took several seconds for Edith to consider and digest this information. As she did, the man began to pick her collars off the pegs one by one. He reached for the first one—Monday's collar—with his greedy, grabby left hand.

"Stick Cat," Edith said, and looked him right in the eyes.

"Yes?"

"I don't like Tuna Todd anymore."

Stick Cat used all his effort to suppress a smile. He knew this was a scary situation, but at this exact moment he was amused that it took something being stolen from Edith herself for her to finally understand the situation.

"I'm sorry about your collars," Stick Cat said. "And I'm sorry Tuna Todd didn't turn out to be as nice as you thought."

"We should have figured it out earlier," hissed Edith.

"Umm," Stick Cat said, and stopped. It seemed like he was contemplating the right words to use. "You're right. If only I had been clever enough to figure out what he was doing."

UMM...

"Don't blame yourself, Stick Cat," Edith said. "Thankfully, you have me here to help."

They both turned to watch the man remove, examine, and take Edith's Monday collar.

"We have to stop him!" Edith exclaimed.

"I know," Stick Cat agreed. "But I don't know how."

The burglar continued to hold Monday's

collar up to the light. He tilted it left and right, and let it dangle in front of his eyes. The collar was decorated with green gemstones. He dropped it into the bag.

"I know how to stop him," Edith said quickly. "We have to call that emergency number on the telephone!"

"You mean 9-1-1?"

"That's it!" Edith exclaimed. She was happy Stick Cat understood. "Quick! What's the number for 9-1-1?!"

"Umm," said Stick Cat. "What do you mean, 'What's the number for 9-1-1?'?"

"That's the emergency number we have to call!"

"Yeah, I know."

"What's the number?" Edith repeated. She was growing more and more exasperated. "What do we dial on the phone?"

"It's, you know, 9-1-1," Stick Cat answered. He couldn't quite comprehend what Edith didn't understand.

"Are you sure?"

"Yes, I'm pretty sure the number for 9-1-1 is 9-1-1," Stick Cat said. "But we can't use a telephone anyway."

"Of course we can," Edith said quickly. She seemed totally frustrated. "I've seen Tiffany use the telephone dozens of times. You pick up the whatchamacallit and press some buttons on the thingamajig and talk into the who-zee-whats-it."

"But the human on the other end won't be able to understand us," Stick Cat explained. This was obvious to him but apparently not yet to Edith. "It won't work."

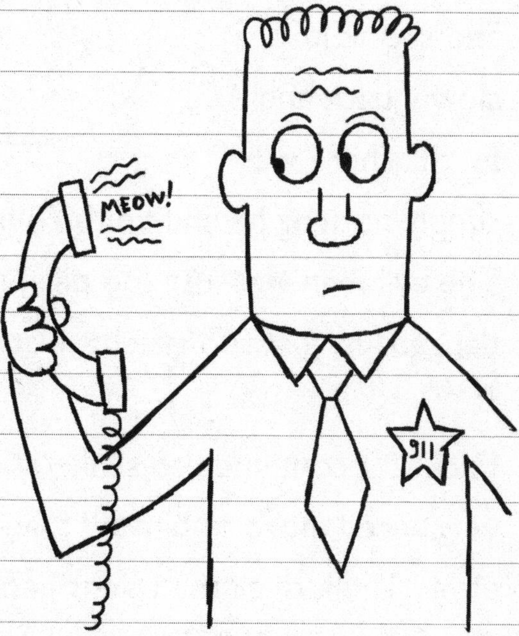
MEOW!
911

In a few seconds, it did dawn on Edith. "Well, of course, it won't. I knew that."

The masked man dropped
Edith's Wednesday collar
into his satchel.

Stick Cat had
almost given up.
He hung his head
and shook it
slowly back and
forth. There was
simply nothing he and Edith could do.
The evil man was just too big. Just too
dangerous. Just too greedy. Just too mean.

Stick Cat continued to shake his head. He
whispered more to himself than anyone
else. "Think of all the things he's taken.
Goose's watch—"

"My collars," Edith included.

"The money for his trip—"

"My collars."

"Tiffany's jewelry."

"My collars."

Stick Cat raised his head and looked at
Edith. While he did, the man dropped Edith's
Thursday collar into his bag of pilfered stuff.

"I'm sorry about your collars," Stick Cat said
sincerely to Edith. "I know they're important
to you."

"They're more valuable than Tiffany's
jewelry, that's for sure."

Stick Cat nodded.

"They're more important than Goose's things—his watch, his trip."

Stick Cat didn't really think Edith's bejeweled collars were more valuable or important than Goose's grandfather's watch or his dream of a special trip to Paris, France. He considered making that point to Edith, but he decided not to for one simple reason.

Do you know what it was?

I'll tell you.

It's kind of an important part of the story.

Something Edith had just said sparked the hint of an idea in Stick Cat's mind. He couldn't quite figure it out yet. But there was something there.

Something.

What was it?

"Edith," Stick Cat
said. "What did
you just say?"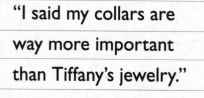

"I said my collars are
way more important
than Tiffany's jewelry."

"No, after that."

"And more important than Goose's things—
his watch, his trip."

That was it.

It was there.

Right there.

"'His watch, his trip,'" whispered Stick Cat.

Edith cocked her head and looked at Stick Cat. "Hunh?"

He repeated, "'Watch, his trip.'"

"Stick Cat? Why are you repeating everything? It's kind of annoying."

And then Stick Cat raised a single eyebrow.

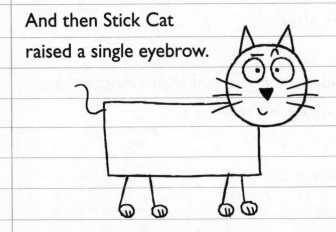

He stared at Edith.

And he said just one thing.

"I know how to stop him."

Edith snapped her head toward Stick Cat.
She stared into his eyes with great intensity.
She really wanted her collars back.

Edith asked, "How?"

Stick Cat smiled and answered, "We're going to *watch* him *trip*."

Chapter 13

EDITH IS BATTY

"Watch him trip?" Edith asked. "What are you even talking about, Stick Cat?"

Stick Cat watched as the man held Edith's Friday collar up to the bedroom light on the ceiling. He admired the red jewels against the light. "Rubies!"

Then he dropped it into the bag.

Stick Cat knew only Edith's Saturday and Sunday collars remained. They didn't have much time.

"We're going to *make* him trip," Stick Cat said urgently. "We need a ball of yarn—fast!"

Edith leaped from the doorway into the bedroom and positioned herself next to a large ball of thick, blue yarn. She batted it toward Stick Cat.

It was a perfect shot.

Stick Cat caught it between his paws and ducked back behind the doorframe, hoping that Tuna Todd had not seen any of this happen.

He hadn't.

He was far too busy admiring the purple flashes and twinkles from the jewels on Edith's Saturday collar.

"Amethyst," he sighed, and dropped the collar into the bag. "Beautiful."

Stick Cat unstrung a good length of yarn from the ball—and waited for Edith to return.

She should have been back by now.

After several seconds, Stick Cat peeked around the doorframe and back into the bedroom.

There was Edith. Right where she was before.

"Edith!" Stick Cat called as quietly as he could.

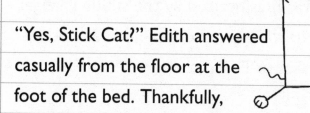

"Yes, Stick Cat?" Edith answered casually from the floor at the foot of the bed. Thankfully, Tuna Todd couldn't see her there. "What can I help you with?"

"What are you doing?!"

"I'm waiting for you," Edith answered.

"But *I'm* waiting for *you!*"

"No, no," Edith said. "You've got it backward. I'm waiting for you."

"Why?" Stick Cat asked as calmly as he could. The masked man seemed almost

155

obsessed with the final collar in his hand.
He twisted Edith's Sunday collar in the light
and was mesmerized by the subtle changes
in its dazzling gemstones. He hadn't noticed
Stick Cat or Edith at all.

"I'm waiting for you to bat the ball of yarn
back, of course!" Edith called. She seemed
dumbfounded that Stick Cat was confused.

"Why?"

"We're cats, that's why," Edith explained
casually. "It's what we're supposed to do."

"But we have to stop Tuna Todd!" pleaded
Stick Cat.

"Balls of yarn, Stick Cat, balls of yarn," Edith
said. "We're cats. We have to bat them

around. We just have to."

Now, this debate would have probably
continued for some time—but it didn't.

That's because at that precise moment, the
masked burglar dropped that final collar into
his satchel. It rattled and clinked
against all the others.

And that noise grabbed
Edith's attention.

"My collars!" she hissed. She remembered
now. And in two sudden bounds she was at
Stick Cat's side.

The masked man had not seen a thing. He
had his back to the doorway as he talked to
himself.

"That's a lot of loot for two apartments," he said, and happily listed all the things he had stolen. He lifted the bag up and down in the air a few times—weighing his bounty. "A pocket watch, a ton of cash, plenty of jewelry, and all these fancy collars. Not bad. Not bad at all!"

While he spoke to himself and enumerated his takings, Stick Cat gave Edith instructions.

"We need you on the other side of the doorway!"

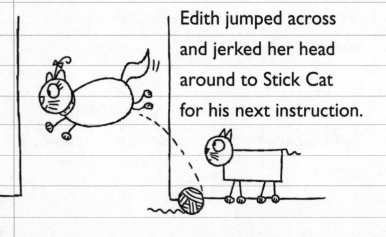

Edith jumped across and jerked her head around to Stick Cat for his next instruction.

"I'll hold this loose end of yarn over here," Stick Cat said as fast as he could.

Edith nodded her understanding.

"You hold the ball on your side," Stick Cat went on quickly. He rolled the yarn ball across to Edith. "When Tuna Todd steps through the doorway, we'll yank the yarn and trip him."

Edith reached for that rolling yarn ball.

Stick Cat shot a glance at the man. He was taking a final look around the room for anything else to steal.

"Get ready. I'm going to pull it tight to trip him right when—"

But he didn't say anything else. That's
because that ball of blue yarn rolled back
across the doorway and bumped into him.
He looked at it.

Edith had batted it back.

Stick Cat yanked his
head up to look at Edith.

She smiled.

She was ready to play.

Stick Cat shook his head
and pushed the ball back

across to Edith. It rolled and tumbled to her.
As it did, Stick Cat said, "No, Edith. I need
you to—"

Too late.

Edith batted it back again.

He looked up at her.

She was still smiling.

"I just LOVE yarn, don't you?" Edith asked.
"I don't love it as much as tuna, mind you.
But yarn is pretty glorious."

Stick Cat shut his eyes
for a split second.

The masked man pivoted in the bedroom. He was ready to leave.

It was no use.

There was no way.

Stick Cat couldn't get Edith to suppress her feline instincts to catch and bat the ball of yarn. She just *HAD* to bat it back. His whole plan was ruined. If Edith didn't hold the other end of the yarn, they couldn't pull it tight to trip Tuna Todd.

Stick Cat could hear the thief's heavy footsteps approaching. He was almost to the doorway.

Stick Cat shook his head slowly in defeat and looked up at Edith.

She was still on the other side of the doorway, sitting back on her hind legs and motioning with her front paws that she wanted Stick Cat to roll the yarn ball back to her.

She wanted to play some more.

Stick Cat gave up.

He rolled the ball of yarn to Edith.

She saw it coming. She smiled and squealed with delight.

She batted it back.

Perfectly.

As Tuna Todd came through the doorway,

that ball of yarn rolled
directly under his foot.

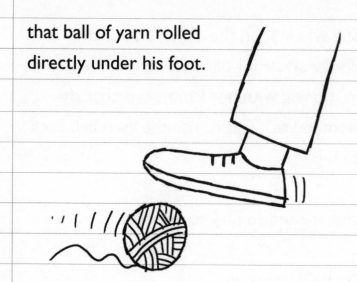

Chapter 14

THUD!

And Tuna Todd fell.

Face-first.

Into the carpet.

Have you ever fallen face-first?

I have.

A bunch of times. I'm pretty good at it.

And do you know what happens when you fall down face-first?

I'll tell you—just in case you're not as experienced in this particular skill as I am.

Here's what happens.

Your instincts kick in.

Your body does what it needs to do faster than your brain can tell your body what to do.

And what does your body do when you fall down face-first?

It throws both of your arms forward to

break the fall.

And here's why that's so important right now.

When Tuna Todd began to fall, his instincts kicked in. His arms flew forward to catch himself. His hands prepared for the impact with the carpet. His fingers stretched out.

And he let go of the bag with the watch, the money, the jewelry, and Edith's collars.

Tuna Todd crashed to the floor in a dull, heavy *THUD!* He bounced against the carpet and fell back onto it with a slightly less dull and slightly less heavy second *THUD!*

By the time the man had bounced and thudded twice, Stick Cat had leaped into the air.

He landed on Tuna Todd's back, bounded off, and touched down right next to the bag.

"You did it, Edith!!" Stick Cat screamed toward Edith as he picked up the bag with his mouth. He began to sprint toward the bathroom. He yelled over his shoulder through clenched teeth, "Come on! Follow me!"

Edith did exactly that.

She soared into the air and smashed down on Tuna Todd's back. She was bigger and heavier than Stick Cat. Edith seemed to enjoy that hard, heavy landing.

"Oomph!" the man yelled.

And Edith jumped off. She landed on the

carpet a few feet away from the man. She turned her head over her shoulder and looked him right in the eye.

"You!" the man screamed, and began to scramble to his feet.

"That's right," Edith answered calmly, and brought a paw up to her collar. She stretched her head and neck a bit in his direction. "It's me. And I got my collars back!"

"Errgh!" the man groaned in both pain and frustration. He was almost to his feet now.

"The bathroom, Edith!" Stick Cat called

from ahead. "Hurry!"

She ran after him.

In the several seconds it took Edith to reach
the bathroom, Stick Cat was already inside
the cabinet. He shoved the bag through their
hole to his and Goose's apartment—and
then jumped through himself. As soon as he
was safely inside the bathroom cabinet on
his side of the wall,
Stick Cat turned
around to look
for Edith.

He heard her before he saw her.

"Here I come!" she screamed.

Stick Cat could hear the masked man's heavy footsteps pound off the living room carpet and onto the tiled bathroom floor. There was no doubt he was gaining speed.

"I see YOU!" the man screamed.

And Stick Cat saw Edith too.

She hurtled toward the cabinet and toward their hole.

Stick Cat had never seen Edith move so fast.

Tuna Todd's footsteps got closer and louder.

"Where are YOU going?!" he thundered. "And WHERE'S that friend of yours?! Where's MY bag?!"

Edith leaped from the bathroom floor, flew into and through the cabinet.

Stick Cat watched wide-eyed.

She was going to make it. Tuna Todd would not be fast enough to catch her.

Edith was airborne.

Her aim was perfect.

Her head came through their hole.

Her shoulders came through.

Her belly did not.

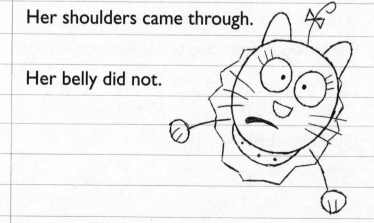

Chapter 15

EDITH HAS A PRETTY TAIL

"Stick Cat!" Edith screamed.

"I see you!" Stick Cat yelled back, and lunged toward her.

"I'm stuck!"

"I know!" Stick Cat answered, and grabbed Edith's front paws. He pulled on his best friend.

But Edith didn't budge.

"I SEE you! And now I'm going to GET you!"
Tuna Todd's muffled voice came booming
from behind Edith. "Just need to GRAB that
pretty tail of yours!"

Edith felt the man's hand brush against her
tail. She swished it away.

As she did, Edith
explained what was
happening behind
her. "He's trying
to grab my tail and
yank me back!"

Stick Cat grasped Edith's front paws as firmly
as he could. He braced his back paws against
the cabinet door's edge.

"He is right, by the way," Edith managed

to say during the crisis. "My tail is quite pretty."

"Just wait until I get hold of YOU!" the man yelled from the other side.

Edith swished her tail out of his grasp again.

Stick Cat yelled, "Get ready!"

"I do pay particular attention to my tail when grooming," Edith said. "It's nice for Tuna Todd to notice. Even though he's a criminal and evil and everything, at least he has excellent taste in tails."

Stick Cat cocked his head at Edith's comment for a split second—and decided not to respond. Instead, he yelled just one simple thing.

"Inhale!"

Edith asked, "Inhale?"

"Inhale!"

"Hunh?"

"Take a deep breath!"

To Stick Cat's great relief, Edith now
understood his directions. She inhaled
deeply.

"I got you NOW!" Tuna Todd bellowed
from the other side. His right hand grasped
the tip of Edith's tail. He squeezed.

And while Tuna Todd pulled from the back,
Stick Cat pulled from the front as hard as
he could. It was a battle between Tuna
Todd and Stick Cat. It tested their strength.
It tested their willpower.

But Stick Cat shared something with Edith
that Tuna Todd did not. Tuna Todd pulled
Edith with revenge and greed in his eyes.
Stick Cat had something else in *his* eyes.

Friendship.

Tuna Todd pulled.

Stick Cat pulled.

Edith's body wriggled.

It shimmied.

And Edith—all of Edith, including her tail—
popped through the hole and tumbled into
Stick Cat's arms.

Because friendship is greater than greed.

friendship > GREED

Chapter 16

EDITH DOES IT AGAIN

Stick Cat couldn't believe it. Edith was there with him. So was the bag of stolen stuff. And Tuna Todd was on the other side of the wall.

"Stick Cat," Edith said.

"Yes?" Stick Cat answered. His arms were still awkwardly wrapped around her. She had popped out of that stuck position with so much force that they had tumbled almost completely out of the cabinet. He was sure Edith was about to thank him for getting her safely to his side before Tuna

Todd pulled her back.
"What is it, Edith?"

"Would you kindly get
your paws off of me?"
she huffed. "You're
messing up my fur."

Stick Cat scrambled
off and away from Edith. "Sorry."

In the few seconds it took for Stick Cat to
untangle himself from Edith, Stick Cat got his
bearings—and observed two very different
things.

First, Edith had made her way over to the
mirror on the back of the bathroom door
and was grooming herself.

Second, Tuna Todd's arm was reaching
through the hole.

"I'd say my tail is more than just 'pretty,'"
Edith declared calmly. Her back faced the
mirror now, and she twisted her head over
her shoulder so she could see the reflection
of her tail. "It's more like 'magnificent' or
'glamorous.' Wouldn't you agree, Stick Cat?"

Stick Cat took a single moment—and three
deep breaths—before answering. He knew
this whole dangerous situation might not be
over. Tuna Todd's arm reached farther and
farther as it probed about inside the cabinet.

"It is magnificent and glamorous, Edith," Stick Cat said quickly. He picked the bag up with his mouth. In the rush to escape with it, Stick Cat hadn't noticed how heavy it was. The collars, money, jewelry, and watch really weighed it down.

Stick Cat looked into the cabinet. The man's arm was no longer there.

But his face was.

He stared through their hole and saw what Stick Cat carried.

"Give me that!" Tuna Todd snarled. "It's MINE!"

He plunged his arm back through the

wall. He stretched as far as he could—
almost reaching the cabinet door with his
fingertips.

Stick Cat stepped back. He—and the bag—
were several inches away from Tuna Todd's
fingers. Stick Cat put the bag down.

"What are you doing?" Edith asked. Now
that she had spent a moment to groom
herself and admire her tail, she seemed
satisfied with her appearance.

"He's trying to reach the bag," answered
Stick Cat. Tuna Todd withdrew his arm and

stared through the hole again. It looked like he was trying to figure out how to reach just a little farther. His eyes were narrowed and laser-focused on the bag. "He really wants to get it back."

"He is NOT getting my collars again," Edith said. "No way."

"Don't worry," said Stick Cat. "He can't fit through our hole. He'll probably just leave here and climb up through the vent in your apartment and escape. Too bad. I wish there was some way to catch him. He'll just steal from somebody else tomorrow. He's so greedy."

"Why does he want my collars in the first place?"

"He thinks they're valuable."

"They wouldn't even fit around his neck. It's ridiculous! And even if he did get one, I bet it would be too tight to get off. He'd be stuck."

"What did you say?" asked Stick Cat. There was the spark of an idea again. He felt it. The fur on his neck popped up just a little bit.

Edith didn't answer. She was now too busy picturing Tuna Todd wearing one of her collars.

"Plus, my collars are not even his style,"

she observed. "He's so plain. All black! All boring, I'd say. No, you need a fanciful, sophisticated personality to wear my collars. You have to be a little *spicy*. You know what I mean?"

"You have, without a doubt, a very spicy personality," Stick Cat said.

Edith liked the sound of this. She closed her eyes about halfway, turned her head a bit to the side, and said, "Yes. Indeed. Quite."

Then Stick Cat asked, "What did you say a minute ago? When you were talking about Tuna Todd wearing your collars?"

"They're not his style?"

"No. Before that."

"A collar would get stuck around his neck."

A peculiar look came to Stick Cat's face
then. A crooked little grin began to grow at
the corner of his mouth.

It wasn't a happy grin.

It was more like a sly grin.

"What is it, Stick Cat?"

"You did it again, Edith," he said. "You did it
again."

"Did what?"

"Solved the problem."

"What problem?"

"How we catch him."

"Catch who?"

"Tuna Todd."

"Oh," Edith said.

"We catch him because he gets stuck."

"How?"

"We use his greed against him," Stick Cat answered. He picked up the bag and winked at Edith. She didn't see him though. Edith had turned around to look in the mirror and admire her tail some more.

Stick Cat took the bag, walked a couple of steps back to the bathroom cabinet, and looked inside.

Tuna Todd wasn't there anymore.

"He's escaping," Stick Cat whispered more to himself than Edith. She was primping her tail.

Stick Cat picked up the bag with his mouth. He turned his head back and forth rapidly, shaking the bag. The collars and jewelry and silver pocket watch clinked and clanked together.

Stick Cat waited.

Edith admired her tail.

And Tuna Todd didn't come back.

Stick Cat shook the bag again.

After waiting several seconds, he shook the bag even more vigorously. The clinking and clanking were significantly louder.

He waited.

Edith admired her tail some more.

Tuna Todd did not come back.

Stick Cat shook the bag one more time—
even harder.

He waited.

Edith admired her tail.

And Tuna Todd came back.

Chapter 17

STUCK

"My bag!" the burglar snarled as he stared through the hole. "Give me that!"

Stick Cat dropped the bag just outside the cabinet door. He knew that spot was just inches out of Tuna Todd's reach.

The man shoved his hand through their hole again. He quickly realized he couldn't reach the bag—and withdrew his arm.

Stick Cat shook the bag again.

Tuna Todd stared through the hole. He had

a serious look on his face. He wanted to solve a problem.

Stick Cat watched him. Even Edith came over from the mirror to watch.

"I want that bag!" the man sneered, and pushed through the hole again.

But this time he pushed through in a different way. This time, he got his shoulder through first and bent and squeezed his arm through after. By using this technique, Tuna

Todd could reach a good bit farther.

But Stick Cat saw it coming.

He grabbed the bag and pulled it farther back.

But not too far.

Tuna Todd's fingertips could reach out of the cabinet now. They wiggled and stretched about in a blind search for the bag.

"Look at his fingers," Edith said. "They look like little sausages."

Stick Cat turned his head sideways to look at Edith.

"What?!" Edith said. "I'm hungry again. They

just reminded me of sausages."

Now, there's something important to know
about this current situation. You see, when
Tuna Todd shoved his shoulder and arm
through the hole, he could not see what
was happening. He had to just feel for the
bag of stolen goods with his hand.

This fact worked to Stick Cat's great
advantage.

And here's how.

Stick Cat took that bag and pushed it just

a little closer—just near enough that the robber could feel it with the very, very, very *tips* of his fingers.

"Errgh!" the man screamed when he realized it was just barely out of reach. His fingers stretched as far as possible. His skin grew tight. He groaned, "Almost . . . got . . . it."

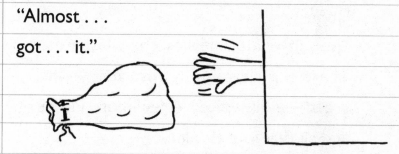

And Stick Cat pulled it a few more inches away.

"Aaah!" the man said. He withdrew his arm and shoulder.

Stick Cat stepped away from the cabinet

door and motioned to Edith to follow him.
She did.

Stick Cat didn't want Tuna Todd to see
them and suspect they were moving the
bag. They stood to the side—out of his
view—and listened as Tuna Todd talked to
himself.

"Just a few more inches," he whispered.
There was clear anger, frustration—and
greed—in his voice. "A few more inches
and all that loot is mine."

Stick Cat and Edith remained out of sight.
And while they couldn't *see* what Tuna Todd
was up to, they could *hear* him quite clearly.

He grunted.

And groaned.

The wall creaked
and strained against
his effort and his weight.

"He's trying to push through!" Edith
exclaimed.

"I know," Stick Cat said, and smiled.

Just then both of Tuna Todd's arms shot out
of the cabinet. They reached the bag and
grasped it.

"A-HA!" Tuna Todd screamed. "I got it! I
GOT it!!"

At the exact moment Tuna Todd's fingers
grasped the bag, Stick Cat sprang into the air

as high as he could. When he reached the apex of his arc—as high as the bathroom sink counter—Stick Cat did two crucial things. First, he checked to ensure his aim was straight and true. It was. He was directly above the bag—and Tuna Todd's hands.

Second, Stick Cat pushed his claws out from his paw pads.

He plummeted down and smacked—claws first—into Tuna Todd's hands.

"AAAGGHH!"

Tuna Todd let go of the bag.

Stick Cat looked inside the cabinet.

Tuna Todd was there. His head, shoulders, and arms were through the hole. The wall was cracked. His pushing had made the hole larger.

"Why you—" the man raged.

Stick Cat smiled at him—and pulled the bag a little farther out of reach.

The man's face was brick red with fury.
He pushed forward harder, wriggling his
shoulders and chest left and right.

Stick Cat pulled the bag a bit farther away.

Tuna Todd continued to wriggle for more
than two whole minutes.

He didn't get anywhere.

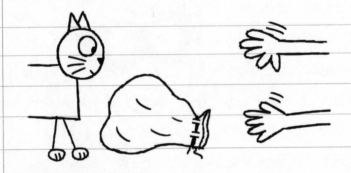

Edith was at Stick Cat's side when she
asked, "What's he doing?"

"He's still trying to reach the bag,"

answered Stick Cat. There was a hint of satisfaction in his voice. It was as if Stick Cat knew his plan was working.

All of Tuna Todd's efforts gained him very little additional reach—maybe two or three inches.

And each time Tuna Todd advanced slightly, Stick Cat pulled the bag a little bit more—keeping it just out of reach.

After eight full minutes, Stick Cat knew his plan had worked. He could tell by the way Tuna Todd's expression had changed. At first, his face was angry and red. Then, for five or six minutes, he looked determined.

But now—just now—Tuna Todd's face had changed once more.

He closed his eyes. His arms fell limp to the cabinet's floor. His head hung.

He was exhausted.

Tuna Todd gave up.

"We got him," Stick Cat said. "He's stuck!"

"He's not even moving," observed Edith.

"He's too tired," Stick Cat replied. "He can't even lift his arms."

"He can't move his arms?" Edith asked. This

piece of information seemed very important to her. "Are you sure?"

"Pretty sure."

And then Edith did something that Stick Cat didn't expect at all. It happened so fast that he didn't even have a chance to stop her.

Edith leaped into the cabinet.

Stick Cat heard a sudden rustling sound.

And as fast as Edith jumped into the cabinet, she jumped out just as quickly.

She had something in her mouth.

She dropped it on the bathroom mat, looked up at Stick Cat, and smiled.

She said just one thing.

"It's tuna time!"

Chapter 18

TWO DIFFERENT PROBLEMS

After they finished eating all the tuna that Edith had snatched from the thief's shirt pocket, she and Stick Cat relaxed on the bathroom mat. The mat was close to the tub. Tuna Todd—still stuck securely in the hole between their bathroom cabinets— could not see them there.

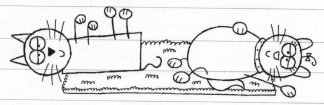

It had been a scary, invigorating, and tiring day.

"We do still have a problem," Stick Cat said to Edith. "You know what it is, right?"

"I think so," Edith said, and licked her whiskers. "We're out of tuna. That's it, right?"

"Umm, no."

"What is it then?"

"There's a man stuck in our hole in the wall."

"It's really quite ridiculous that he's stuck in that hole, don't you think?" Edith asked Stick Cat.

"How so?"

"Well, you know, stuck in a wall," explained Edith. "There's a reason he's stuck. I mean, he should probably lose a few pounds, get some exercise, and make better choices at mealtime."

Stick Cat turned away from Edith then. He didn't want her to see him smile. There was not the tiniest hint of irony in her voice. Edith didn't make any connection whatsoever with that hole and being stuck there many times herself. Once Stick Cat had stifled his laugh and was certain he had control of himself, he turned back to face Edith directly.

"You're right," Stick Cat said. "It is kind of ridiculous. But with him stuck in the wall we have a predicament on our paws."

Edith tilted her head.

"What's the problem?"

"You can't get back to your
apartment."

"I see. Yes."

"We'll be caught by Goose and Tiffany."

"Correct."

"They will probably plug up the hole."

"Right."

"We won't be able to get together every day."

Edith nodded.

"That's a real problem," Stick Cat said. He tried to maintain a calm expression and demeanor on the outside, but the prospect of not spending time with Edith made him incredibly sad on the inside.

Edith looked directly at Stick Cat.

She said, "I still think running out of tuna is a bigger problem."

Stick Cat smiled—but just for a moment.

That's because right then a clear and distinct noise came from the living room.

The dead bolt lock on the door clicked.

The doorknob turned.

Goose was home.

Chapter 19

GOOSE MEETS EDITH

It only took a few seconds for Goose to realize what had happened. There were clues everywhere.

Stick Cat followed Goose around as he discovered each piece of information. Edith waited in the bathroom. She was fluffing her tail with her tongue. She wanted to look her best.

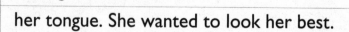

The air-conditioning vent cover was on the

living-room floor.

The dresser drawers were all open in the bedroom and sock balls were scattered all over the place.

The lid was off the cookie jar in the kitchen—and all his Paris, France, money was gone.

Goose picked up Stick Cat and held him close.

"We got robbed, I guess, hunh? Were you scared?" Goose asked. "None of this matters. I'm just glad you're okay."

Stick Cat purred to let Goose know that

he was fine. And then Stick Cat nodded his head toward the bathroom.

"There's more? Is that what you're trying to tell me? They took stuff from my bathroom too?" Goose asked, and smiled a bit. He set Stick Cat down on the floor. "What did they take? My shampoo?"

Of course, what Goose found in the bathroom was not a missing shampoo bottle.

No.

What he found were three very different things.

The first thing he found was Edith. She was still primping in front of the mirror when Stick Cat and Goose walked in.

"Who do we have here?" Goose asked when he saw her. He looked back and forth a couple of times between Edith and Stick Cat. "Hmm. This is getting stranger and stranger with each passing minute."

Edith turned toward Goose, batted her eyes, and returned to examining herself in the mirror.

"This is a friend of yours, I assume?" Goose asked Stick Cat.

Stick Cat purred.

"Okay, then," Goose said, and glanced toward Edith. "She sure is pretty."

Edith turned instantly and caught Stick Cat's attention. "I like your roommate," she said. "He has excellent taste. That is obvious."

"Yes, he does," replied Stick Cat as he nudged the satchel full of stuff toward Goose. The bag bumped up against his right foot.

This was the next thing Goose discovered.

"What's this?" Goose asked as he picked up the bag and opened it. He peered inside and saw his grandfather's pocket watch, lots of loose money, Tiffany's jewelry, and Edith's collars.

Goose shook his head.

"I don't underst—" he began to say, but then stopped himself. He looked at Edith and saw her fancy collar. And then he looked into the bag and saw Edith's six other fancy collars. He looked at her and asked, "Are these yours? How—"

But Goose didn't get to ask another question.

Do you know why?

It's because right then he discovered the third thing.

A tired, weak, and raspy voice called out

from inside the bathroom cabinet.

"Help!" Tuna Todd called in a low whisper.
"I'm stuck."

Goose stooped down to look into the
bathroom cabinet and make his third
discovery. He saw Tuna Todd.

Goose didn't say a word.

But Tuna Todd did.

"Call the police," the robber begged. "Call
a plumber. Call anybody! I don't care. I just

want to get out of this wall!"

Goose nodded and reached into his pocket
to retrieve his phone. He called the police.

Chapter 20

THAT'S TOTALLY GROSS

Over the next hour, many things happened that led to one life-changing event.

It was a life-changing event for Stick Cat.

And for Edith.

And for Goose.

And for Tiffany.

Here's what happened in that next hour.

The police came to Goose and Stick Cat's

apartment. Tiffany came home and met the police in the hallway. The police explained who Tuna Todd was, what he had done, and that he was stuck in the wall. After a lot of pulling, tugging, and yanking on Tuna Todd's feet, the police took Tuna Todd away.

When the police were gone, Edith climbed back through the wall.

And that's when the life-changing thing happened.

Tiffany and Edith looked through the hole in the wall from their side. And Goose and Stick Cat looked through the hole from their side at the same time.

"I'm Goose,"
said Goose.

"I'm Tiffany," said Tiffany.

"I think I have your
jewelry over here,"
Goose said,
and lifted the bag for
Tiffany to see. He
shook it a little. "And
I have your cat's collars too, I think. They're
pretty fancy."

Tiffany smiled. "She's a pretty particular cat.
Her name is Edith."

223

There was silence then.

It was not an awkward silence.

Something else was happening.

Tiffany stared at Goose.

Goose stared at Tiffany.

Stick Cat and Edith stared at their roommates.

"What are these two doing?" Edith asked Stick Cat.

Stick Cat whispered his reply. It was almost as if he didn't want to interrupt something.

He answered, "I think I know."

"Well, what is it?" Edith asked again impatiently. "What are they doing?"

"They're starting to like each other," replied Stick Cat.

Edith thought about this idea for a moment. Then she told Stick Cat exactly what she thought about it.

She said, "That's totally gross."

"It is gross, I agree," Stick Cat answered. And then he smiled. Something else had occurred to him. "But it might mean we can continue to play together."

"I like that idea," Edith admitted.

Tiffany twitched her head a little bit, shaking herself out of her own stare.

"I'm sorry," she said to Goose. "All the excitement has me a bit flustered. Did you say you have my jewelry and Edith's collars?"

Goose nodded. "Would you like to come over and get them?"

"I'd like that," said Tiffany.

Stick Cat purred to get Goose's attention.

"Oh," he said. "And can you bring Edith?"

"Of course," Tiffany said. "Wouldn't it be nice if they became friends?"

THE END

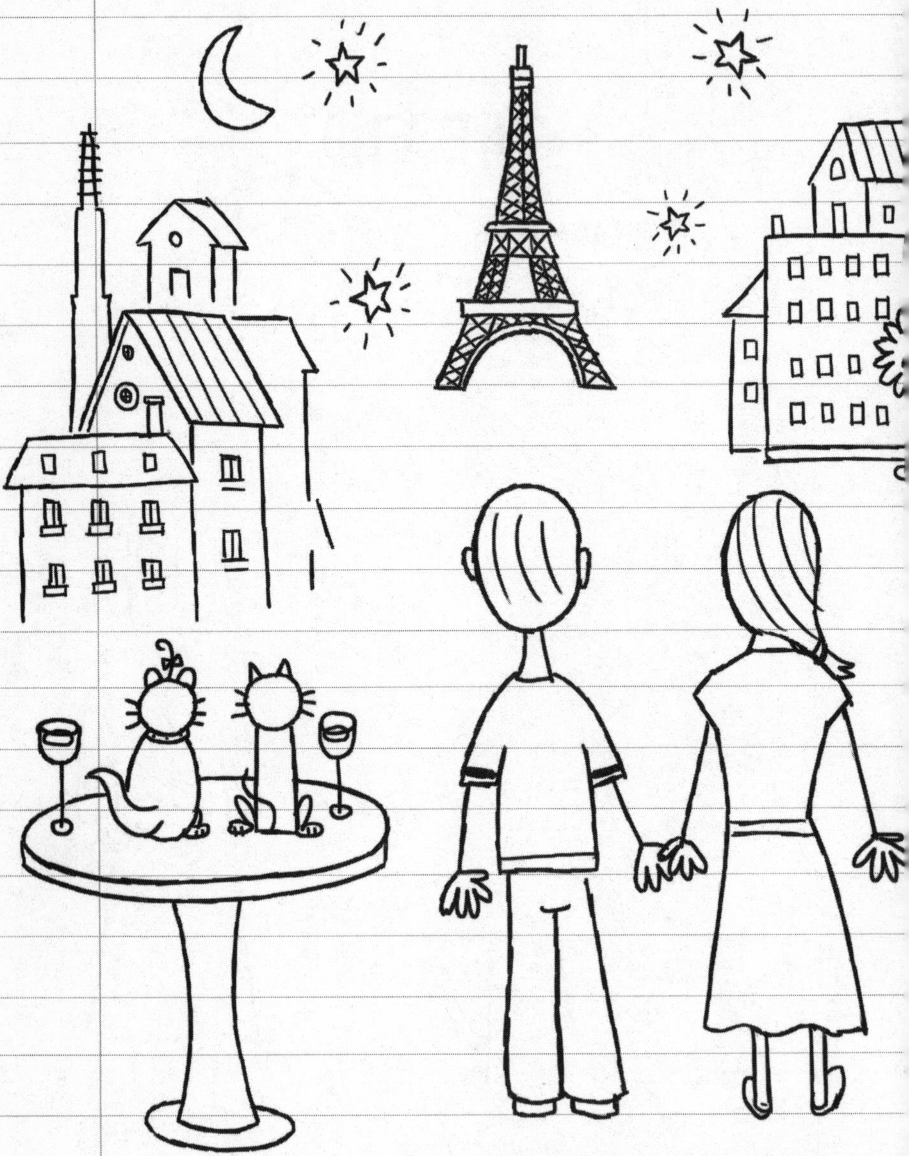

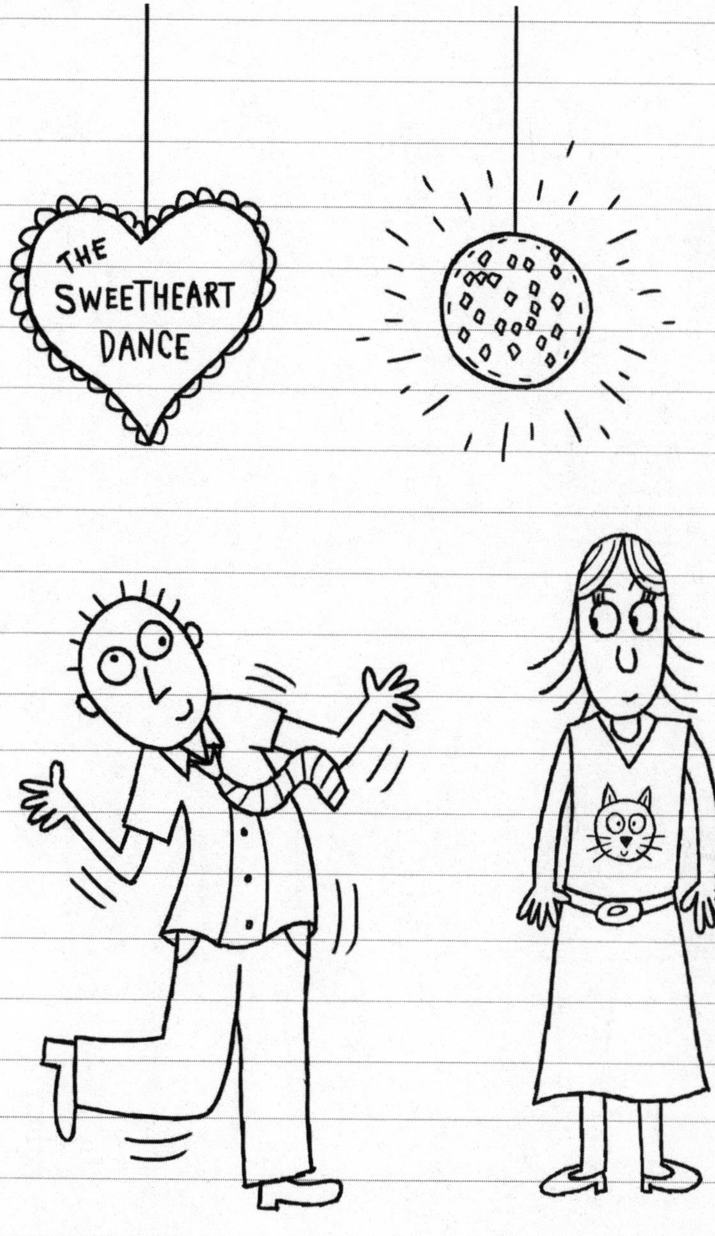
THE SWEETHEART DANCE

Tom Watson is the author of the Stick Dog series. There are currently seven books in that series—and more to come.

He lives in Chicago with his wife, daughter, and son. He also has a dog, as you could probably guess. The dog is a Labrador-Newfoundland mix. Tom says he looks like a Labrador with a bad perm. He wanted to name the dog "Put Your Shirt On" (please don't ask why), but he was outvoted by his family. The dog's name is Shadow. Shadow gives Tom lots of ideas for the Stick Dog series.

Tom Watson is also the author of the Stick Cat series.

Tom does not have a cat. So his ideas for the Stick Cat series come from a whole different place. He's not sure where that place is exactly, but he knows it's kind of strange there.

Visit him online at stickdogbooks.com!

Also available as an ebook.

STICK WITH READING!

STICK DOG
Tom Watson
a really GOOD story with kind of BAD drawings
STICK DOG
WANTS A HOT DOG
Tom Watson
Another really GOOD story with kind of BAD drawings
STICK DOG
CHASES A PIZZA
Tom Watson
STICK DOG
DREAMS OF ICE CREAM
Tom Watson
STICK DOG
TRIES TO TAKE THE DONUTS
Tom Watson
Dizzy's Donuts
STICK DOG
SLURPS SPAGHETTI
Tom Watson
STICK DOG
CRAVES CANDY
Tom Watson
STICK CAT
By Tom Watson
Author of Stick Dog
A Tail of Two Kitties
STICK CAT
By Tom Watson
Author of Stick Dog
Cats in the City
STICK CAT
By Tom Watson
Author of Stick Dog
Two Catch A Thief

Pick up these animal adventures
by Tom Watson today!

Visit www.stickdogbooks.com for

HARPER

An Imprint of HarperCollins*Publishers*